Werev
IN SP
A Science Myt
Sean M. T. :

GW01033084

---

1. http://www.seanmts.com

For more information, address:

FIRST EDITION

a novella sampling of
Tales of the Lunar Launch Team
by Joseph Smith

Table of Contents

Table of Contents

Part 1: Containment Breach

THE BEASTS HAD HIS scent, and now they were loose.

A bloodcurdling scream echoed throughout the facility's clinical hallways, followed by a horrendous howl.

"Shit." Felix huddled into a maintenance nook as a hulking figure stalked around the corner at the end of the hallway. The shape was silhouetted in the dimness by the strobing amber alarm light. *Did it see me?* He curled up against the circuitry in the wall, shuddering with every step of the creature as it drew closer. All the while it was sniffing, huffing, and growling. The lower gravity muted its approach, but could not hamper the sickening click and scrape of claw upon metal.

There was a spine-shrinking shriek as it tore its foreclaws down the wall. Felix attempted to stifle an involuntary gasp, and the shrieking stopped; the beast homed in on his hidey-hole. There were two quick, shuddering steps and Felix caught the dank smell of its misted breath, which reflected in the dusky light. Sinister claws reached around the edges of the nook.

Felix screamed, "Computer, activate breach suppression!"

Jets of steam billowed from vents in the ceiling, sparkling with trace amounts of silver metal, and the beast roared. Felix only had an instant to act. He held his breath and dashed from his hiding spot, tearing away from the howling monster that filled the hallway, and bolted for the maintenance control room just down the next hall.

The jets of silver steam fizzled out after only an instant, and the flailing beast turned to sight its prey.

"Too soon, too soon, fuck!" Felix muttered curses as he fumbled for his security pass. He swiped the side panel and the door slid open. Bolting inside, he hit the emergency lock and the doors groaned closed with horrible slowness. All the while, the beast galloped down the narrow hallway, intending to disembowel him. As the doors clenched shut, Felix made eye contact with his hunter. Yellow bloodshot orbs gazed right into his soul with hunger and fury.

The doors hissed shut and Felix found himself trembling, feet rooted to the spot. The door shuddered and he leaped back with a scream . . . but they held, even as the beast raked them from the other side and howled in frustration.

Felix allowed himself a sigh of relief.

"Hello, fren!" Felix jumped in fright again as a small furry creature scurried out from under a workbench and hopped up to greet him. "It's hecking scary out there!"

"Floof!" Felix laughed and patted the frightened mastiff. "You scared the shit out of me!"

The dog licked Felix's face, and the collar around its neck lit up as the neural translator converted its thought patterns into an adorable, electronic voice. "There are toothy boys out there!"

"That damned dog scared the shit out of me too."

"Fuck, Helena!" Felix pushed past Floof to help the woman who was wedged under the workbench Floof was hiding under.

She wore a white lab coat; her hair was short and frizzy, and bobbed in the low-G. "Shit, you're bleeding. Did they . . ."

"It was just broken glass, don't worry." She batted away his hands. "How did they get out, Felix?"

"The cell doors just opened. It can't have been a malfunction, I think we have a mole," Felix said.

"A mole?" Helena stiffened. "But why? This is a research facility to treat . . ." she trailed off as Felix gave her a deadpan look. "All right, that might have been naive on my part, but who?"

"I don't know. Whoever it is, they sabotaged the suppression systems. I couldn't use it to save the others. I could barely use it to save myself. Whoever sabotaged us must have gotten to them too. All that doesn't matter for the moment, we need to get out of this. I'm glad we had the same idea—did you manage to send out a distress signal?"

Helena eyed the console by the plexiglass observation section of the maintenance room—a bulky rover sat outside, inert on the chalky grey surface of the Moon. The screen had an indicator blinking: '*MESSAGE SENT.*'

"Yes, but that's no use to us; it'll take half a day for a rescue squad capable of dealing with this kind of situation to arrive. We need to escape, but we can't make it to the rover unless we clear the way. Now that you're here, we can do something to get rid of the escaped subjects."

"Like what?" Felix helped Helena up onto her feet.

"I had a plan before you opened the door and scared me under the table. I was going to send Floof through this vent here. It leads to the airlock corridor. I was going to smear my blood on him and send him through to draw them in. Then I was going to seal the corridors with the maintenance control overrides from this console and vent the airlock, launching the subjects out onto the Moon's surface."

"You were going to vent Floof?" Felix gasped.

"No, I was going to call him back into the vent and seal it. They won't stay in the hallway once they realise it's just him anyway. The only thing is, the damned dog won't go!"

"I am too spooked!" Floof barked.

"It's okay, buddy," Felix tousled the dog's ears and swallowed the lump in his throat. "I'll go."

"You can't!" Helena protested, but Felix placed his hand on her shoulder, squeezing it. "Will you even fit?" she said.

"I've been on a diet." Felix slapped his belly, but his smile was strained. "Look after Floof while I'm gone, yeah?"

The door shuddered with another sickening howl and the three occupants of the room leaped back in fright.

"That's my cue," Felix said. He grabbed one of the radios racked on the wall, shuffled under the desk, and popped open the vent cover. After a moment's hesitation, he crawled inside. "I'll speak to you on the maintenance channel."

"Be careful out there," Helena whispered after him, taking her own radio from the wall rack.

"Hey, you're talking to Felix Hernandez here, I once killed a tarantula with a . . ."

"With a blow dart, yes," Helena laughed. "I've heard the story a dozen times."

Felix shuffled further into the vent, finding himself in a narrow, dark, cramped, and dusty shaft. After a few moments of exerted crawling, he saw thin strips of strobing amber light through the next vent cover. He cracked it open, poked half of his dust covered head out of the vent, and found the dark corridor. The amber alarm lights were mounted to the ceiling on either end; the terrible rumbling of the monsters as they tore through the facility, looking for prey, was ever-present.

Felix pulled himself out of the vent and turned on the radio. He held it up to his mouth with trembling hands and clicked the transmission button. The sharp static was enough to make him flinch, but he held to his resolve. "Helena, I'm in the hallway. Open all doors and hatches that lead to my location. I'm ready when you are."

The hissing clank of doors opening sounded throughout the base, and then Helena's reply came in a static-charged whisper. "I'm ready. Good luck."

"Just be ready to seal the vent quickly." Felix took a deep breath, and then started banging on the walls, yelling at the top of his lungs. "Come and get me!"

His stomach twisted as a cascade of howls echoed throughout the base, followed by snarling and growling. Some of the sounds were disturbingly close by. As the clacking of claw on metal and rumbling of great beasts converging on his location grew closer, the noise was accompanied by the sound of closing doors and hatches. Felix wiped the sweat off his brow and decided that meant they were in the adjacent corridors, and Helena had sealed them in.

He turned toward the vent and popped open the grating; the emergency compression barrier slid down on the other side, an impenetrable slab of metal.

A fevered panic rose up Felix's spine. He kicked in the emergency vent seal and tried to tear at its edges with his fingertips as a snarl harbingered the pack of monsters rounding the corner to the airlock corridor. The werewolves had found him.

Felix desperately keyed the radio, "Helena, the vent is sealed! I'm trapped in the hallway!"

As the beasts prowled into the corridor, leering closer to feed upon him, Helena's cool voice responded. "I am aware, Doctor Hernandez."

"Helena," Felix said. His racing heart threatened to explode, but he knew he would not be lucky enough to experience such a clean death. "What the fuck are you doing?"

"Oh, for an agent of the Pantheon, you don't catch on very quickly," Helena answered as dread dawned over Felix. "The Cronos Sect sends their regards."

Felix's fearful grip kept the radio clicked on as the pack of werewolves finally broke rank, tearing into the hallway to rip him limb from limb. "You . . ." his final words were interrupted by a torrent of curses in Spanish and screams of anguish.

From her relative safety, Helena viewed the frenzy through the grainy security camera feed she had brought up on the maintenance console. Felix's curses were accompanied by the sound of howls, snapping bone, and the wet wrenching of sinew. She waited, hovering with her finger over the emergency vent button to really twist the knife.

Floof barked, "I sure hope Felix is okay! Toothy boys are multiplying out there!"

Helena frowned. "Let's turn off the kid's setting for now." She flicked a setting on the collar, and Floof's voice changed from a dopey tone to a monotone computer narrated voice.

"Hostile creatures have overwhelmed the base," Floof said.

"Yes, I know that . . ."

"Danger imminent, danger imminent, danger imminent."

"For fuck's sake," Helena answered, and tuned out the dog's droning warning. She focused back on the console. Felix was still alive somehow, screaming as the werewolves ate their fill. Amongst the horrid cacophony, she realised Felix was still screaming profanities. She heard the Spanish word for *'whore'* and smirked, then finally, mercifully, vented the airlock.

The whole station rocked. The grainy security feed became a turbulent blur as the escaped test subjects, Felix's body, and the trapped air in the adjacent corridors was violently expelled into the vacuum of the Moon's surface.

"Danger imminent, danger imminent . . ."

"You still droning on about that, you stupid dog?" Helena sighed, "They're all vented! For fuck's sake, I'll tear that neural link out of you if you don't shut the hell up!" Floof recoiled with a whimper, but his message remained constant and monotone.

"Have it your way! First I need to make sure the distress signal reaches the right ears . . ." she went over to the console by the plexiglass viewing platform, only to gasp.

Out on the Moon's surface, the beasts were thrashing about amongst the debris of decompression. They were still alive, and bounding back to the airlock in a slow-motion manner that would have looked comical if it weren't so terrifying. Their skin was shrivelled back around their faces, and blood and bodily fluids were siphoning from every orifice in a half-boiled jet stream.

It was pure madness.

"Oh, fuck!"

Five of the test subjects reached the airlock, and the sixth bounded over to the glass and leered in at her. Its eyes were even more bloodshot; the drool was still being sucked from its snarling snout even as it produced more to keep its mouth moist, and it started raking down the glass with ferocious tenacity. "Jesus!" Helena shrieked back.

"...danger imminent..."

The doors to the maintenance control room—which led to one of the corridors that was vented—shuddered as the beasts reached it and started clawing their way in.

Helena scanned the room, looking for something—anything—to help her out of this impossible situation. All the while, the beasts, the werewolves, clawed their way through the thick vacuum shielding. And all the while, Floof continued his incessant, droning warning.

"...danger imminent, danger imminent, danger imminent ..."

Part 2: The Griffins

BHANU EVERLY

Counter Paranormal task force - G.R. – F.I.N: *Global Response – Fable Infringement Necessity*

. . . PRIORITY TRANSMISSION . . .

Mission briefing directed to: Captain Bhanu Everly

Highest priority orders: Redirect from Orbital Spire Station to Lunar Colony 'Amenitude' and meet United Globe liaison for classified intelligence. Proceed to mission actual from there.

Mission priorities:

1. Seek and destroy

2. Retrieve classified data

3. Search and rescue

G.R. - F.I.N. Command.

Bhanu reread the message for the tenth time, murmuring her vexations over the lack of intel. Even that small movement hurt her chapped brown lips. She licked them instinctively—and regretted it immediately.

"Fucking space flight," she said, and smacked her lips.

Her foul language didn't mesh with her posh accent, she realised with a suppressed smirk. Lucas had rubbed off on her.

"Say something, Ev?" Lucas turned from the flight console, his beard scuffing against his microphone and causing her to wince with the sudden burst of static.

"Dude!" his co-pilot Roshni winced as well. "How the hell do you get away with that face scruff as a GR operative?"

"Well, I was gonna shave it but I cannae dunnit now that we didn't have time at dock. You ever shave in the bathroom on this vessel? You're asking for clogged vents, you stupid wee lass!"

Bhanu's smile grew in spite of her cracking lips. Roshni had been Lucas's co-pilot for only a week, and had settled into his abrasive style easily. And he . . . *Well, he's recovering quickly from the incident,* Bhanu thought. *It's no small feat to pull through the trauma of having your co-pilot impaled right next to you. Christ, the squad has taken some hits recently.*

The console chimed and the three occupants of the cockpit looked out through the quartz glass screen. The Moon now filled most of their field of view, spinning as their vessel flew in a corkscrew path to maintain a sense of gravity through inertia. The Moon was grey and desolate—save for the sporadic lighting of colonies and flashes of orbital traffic—and marred by garish craters. Some thought it lost its lustre the closer you got, but Bhanu found it pretty all the same. They crossed the proximity threshold and were now able to receive docking instructions.

"How long until we dock, Lucas?"

"Half an hour, Cap'n," Lucas answered. "This lot are demanding."

"How so?"

"The Lunar Government has strict weapons controls." Roshni was flicking through the data package on her tablet. "We can't take our firearms into Amenitude, and seeing as it's armed, the Hippogriff will be grounded once we dock."

"Hey there, let's call in a paranormal spec ops unit for what I can only assume is a highly dangerous situation, but have them come out with fisticuffs!" Lucas laughed.

"Bloody lunar bureaucracy," Roshni tutted.

"More like *lunacy,* am I right?" Lucas said.

Bhanu rolled her eyes even though she was still smiling. "Just proceed with docking, and ping the FNG while you're at it. I want to have a word with him."

"Ma'am," Lucas grinned, flicked some switches on the console, and spoke into his microphone, "Oi, Fucking New Guy, Cap'n wants a word! The rest of ya, prepare for a flaccid man's version of real grav!" He flicked off the switch and continued correcting his course.

"As professional as ever, Lucas."

"I stick by stringent standards, Cap'n Ev." Lucas said seriously, before a wry grin broke through his scruffy visage.

"How come you don't give me the kind of shit you give the new guy?" Roshni asked.

"I've been giving ya shit, ye'r just so dumb ye cannae notice!"

Roshni chuckled, "If that's what you call giving shit, then I have low hopes for this partnership."

"Partnership? Blimey, we're not married!"

Bhanu ignored the brewing banter and stepped out of the cockpit. As the door slid shut behind her, she was confronted by the FNG, who was standing to attention.

"Private Diondre Harris," she said slowly, "that was fast."

"I'm eager to please, ma'am." He spoke with a rigid and formal American accent. He was a young man, and tall, with dark umber skin and a strong, clean-shaven jaw. The black and bronze Griffin fatigues accented his athletic features, but they did not yet suit him—not in her eyes.

"We're close to making Moon-fall. I'd like you to round up the Griffins, as the liaison will be expecting us immediately."

"Yes, ma'am!" Diondre turned to obey, but hesitated. "Ma'am, why not just ping the whole squad?"

Bhanu eyed the young soldier for a moment. "I wanted to have a word with you in private, Diondre . . ."

"Ah, Captain Everly, G.R. guidelines state that we shouldn't . . ."

"That's entirely the problem. You're too formal, too eager to be here, to fit in with how you *think* things are done. You're filling the shoes of someone the squad was well accustomed to and you're acting so formally it's as if you're spitting on his memory."

"Captain, I mean no disrespect . . ."

"Look, it's not your fault, it's just politics. The Americans were next in line to select an agent for the Griffins. But we didn't even get a chance to vet you or the other candidates before the distress signal cocked things up. We had some time with Roshni, and with you, none at all. Don't be surprised if the team takes a while to warm up to you. Many of them would rather charge into the unknown while down a member than have the unknown fighting alongside them. The squad doesn't think you belong here; that's what I'm saying. Hell, the team didn't even meet you until we stepped onto the Hippogriff."

"Ma'am . . . Bhanu, with all due respect, I busted my ass to be a Griffin."

"And yet you have no previous experience with the paranormal. Everyone on this team had more than military experience before they joined. Hell, one of them didn't have any military training at all. But they have all had encounters with the unknown, they have all stared into the abyss, and they're still alive. They resent someone like you. I just wanted to let you know they're watching. Don't cock it up."

Diondre considered this for a moment, "Understood, ma'am, I'll do my best."

"That's all I can ask. Now, go round up the squad. And cut that military discipline out. It won't work with this outfit. Griffins are notoriously irreverent, and for good reason."

"Ma'am . . . I mean . . ."

"Just call me Bhanu or Ev, Diondre. Move out."

KIERAN AHMAD

Kieran bowed over the prayer mat, murmuring to himself in Arabic. Then he rose to his knees and gazed out the observation window, to the tiny blue dot spinning in the wake of the Hippogriff. The Hippogriff was a specialised AC-APC: Aerospace Capable - Armoured Personnel Carrier. It had limited living functions for longer operations outside Earth's atmosphere, including bunk cabins, a mess and the observation deck at the rear of the ship, a tiny little closet space that Kieran utilised for his prayers.

It was a tiny enough compartment that he could feel Aideen's nervous energy as she waited for him to finish. It was like a static charge in the air. He tried to ignore it, but Aideen always demanded to be noticed.

The two Griffins could not be more different. Kieran was broad and bulky, with dark olive skin and a short cropped beard that hugged his square jaw. In contrast, Aideen was pale, with bright red hair. She was slight, shorter and leaner than Kieran by a large margin, but held herself in a way that warned she could more than make up for her size with her fighting spirit.

She also did not possess an ounce of reverence for Kieran's prayers.

"So, Kieran," she said as she leaned against the wall and crossed her arms. Kieran touched his head to the mat and came up again to finish his prayer. "You done there?" she asked. Her thick Irish accent had her th's pronounce as t's.

"Yip," Kieran braced himself for Aideen's well meaning chatter as he gently rolled up his mat, his words clipped by a crisp New Zealand accent.

"That's good then, 'cause I have some questions that have been troubling me since we started vacuum training."

"And what's that, Aideen?"

"Well, you have to face west when you pray right, or east? Doesn't matter which-where you need to face, 'cause out here there is no east, nor west, nor up nor down, you follow?"

Most would have a hard time following her fast speech, but Kieran understood through sheer force of experience.

"We face towards the Kaaba in Mecca when we pray, towards the setting sun," he pointed at the spinning blue dot, "So no, no problems on that front. I can't not face Mecca when looking at the planet." He stowed his mat away within the cramped compartment.

"Yeah, but, what if we couldn't see Earth? What if Lucas is doing fancy flying manoeuvres like twirly whirlies or we're behind the Moon? Or even *on* the Moon . . . would you face up, down? What do you do in a situation like that?"

"Far out, Aideen! I can only do my best and that seems to be good enough! But if I'm really stuck, I use this." He produced a little brown cube with a screen set into the top displaying a digital gyroscopic compass. It twisted and turned in tandem with the Hippogriff's pirouetting path. "This is set to track a satellite that orbits around Earth. As long as it's charged it tells me where to look, up to a distance somewhere out past Mars, I think. All I have to do is look at this and do my best from there to point myself towards Earth."

Aideen whistled. "That there is fancy . . ."

Someone cleared their throat, and Kieran and Aideen both looked to the entrance of the observation room, where Diondre was standing stiffly.

"Well fuck me, here I am asking stupid questions and I get some pleb listening in on me!" she stormed past Diondre and out of the observation deck.

"Captain Everly wants us ready at the loading bay, pronto!" Diondre called after her, he looked back to Kieran who was chuckling. "Did she call me a . . . pleb?"

"Don't take her too seriously for the moment, new guy." Kieran clapped him on the shoulder with a meaty hand. "She and Jason . . ." Kieran's dark eyes turned distant for a split second before he continued. "Well, she and he were quite close. Seeing you standing there so soon is like seeing you standing on his grave."

Diondre nodded. "Damn, that minotaur really did a number on you guys."

"Oh, the minotaur took Monica out of commission for a while—Lucas's old co-pilot—but something else got Jason."

"That's not what the reports said," Diondre commented, raising an eyebrow.

"Walk with me, new guy."

"Diondre."

"Yeah, whatever," Kieran replied, waving him off as they moved through the mess hall to the elevator that Aideen had just taken down to the cargo hold.

Within the mess, two other Griffins were locked in a grappling match, scattering serving trays and rations about the place.

One of the Griffins got the upper hand—a tall, pale woman with bright blonde hair. She pinned her comrade, a squat man with short, dark hair, to the table. "Spit it out!" she barked, "That was *my* bacon, Isao! Spit it out!"

Isao laughed. With his face pressed against the table, he uttered something that sounded like, "Snooze you lose!"

"Solvi, Isao!" Kieran barked.

The distraction was enough for Isao to dislodge Solvi; he swallowed the bacon in his mouth, "Victory! What's up, Kieran?"

"Didn't the new guy tell you that Ev wants us in the cargo hold?" Kieran crossed his arms.

"Well, maybe, but . . ." Isao gestured at Diondre, pointing at him with another rasher of bacon, "he's the new guy?" Isao grunted as Solvi saw the bacon flapping in his hands and elbowed him.

"We'll be ship-shape in time, Kieran, don't you worry!" Solvi got Isao's arm into a lock and started yelling at him in

Norwegian. Isao just smiled under her onslaught as he chewed on some new morsel.

"Well," Kieran said, watching the grappling match in amusement as Diondre stared on, gobsmacked. "Be down there in five minutes. And I don't want to hear Lucas bitching about having to clean this place up while we're on mission."

"Sure thing, Kieran!" Isao wriggled out of Solvi's arm lock and the brawl fell off the table onto the floor.

"And keep that pig meat away from my . . ."

"Yes, yes!" Solvi grunted. "Five minutes, clean up afterwards."

"Right," Kieran nodded to Diondre and they made their way to the elevator. "Now, what was I saying before those two interrupted us . . . ah." He hit the call button on the elevator to take them down to the loading bay. "Tell me, new guy, are you a religious man?"

"Can't say that I am, Sergeant."

"Just call me Kieran, we aren't proper military."

"I've been gathering that."

"But yeah, few Griffins are religious, facing the horrors that they do. My faith keeps me grounded though, as Aideen's and Bhanu's does them. I can't speak for them, but for me, the horrors are just things—awful things, but things nonetheless. Having faith, something to ground me in what's important, in what's worth fighting for, it helps. I know the risks when facing those things, and so did Jason. This makes it easier to cope when a thing of mythos claims a member of our ranks. But something else got him, and that's what's really riled us up."

"So the report that said Jason was killed by the minotaur—it was falsified?" Diondre asked.

Kieran gave him a look. "There is another organisation out there that operates in the same sphere as us. They don't leave evidence, but I am certain that they got Jason. Send us after eldritch horrors, sure. But when Griffins talk about shadowy people who leave no trace, Command gets itchy and retires those agents for psychological reasons."

"So why tell me?"

"Because trust swings both ways, brother." The elevator doors slid open and Kieran gestured for him to enter. "We're all on the same team now, whether the others like it or not. If we don't trust each other, we're as good as dead."

The Hippogriff shuddered as Lucas turned out of their corkscrew path and sailed into the lunar gravity well.

"Noted, Kieran."

"And don't worry about the others, they'll come around. And if they don't, well, you're fucked anyway."

Part 3: Lunacy

KIERAN AHMAD

The Griffins dealt with the nausea of shifting from inertial based gravity to the light lunar-G with relative ease, due to their intense psychological training. After assembling in the cargo hold, they forwent donning their tactical gear due to the local restrictions and half marched—half bounded—down the Hippogriff's loading ramp into the Moon base hangar. Lucas and Roshni stayed behind to maintain their ship.

The hangar was a colossal enclosed space lined with vessels and cordoning light markers that directed hovering traffic to and from the huge cycling airlocks at the entrance. A man waited for them upon the black steel flooring, under the control tower half set into the hangar wall. He wore a full space suit—despite the fact the hangar was pressurised—with reflective fluoro colouring that shone brightly under the harsh ceiling lights.

"G'day," he said with an exaggerated wave to account for his bulky suit.

"Just my luck," Kieran chirped as he bobbed like a deflating balloon, stopping himself awkwardly in the low-G when Bhanu ordered them to halt, "an Australian."

Their liaison turned to Kieran and a smug smile shone through his tinted dome helmet. "A Kiwi! Still salty about the rugby?"

"Who won the cricket again?" Kieran shot back.

"Gentlemen!" Bhanu snapped. Kieran and the liaison stood to attention. "I did not know we would need vacuum gear on this mission, officer."

The Australian shrugged. "Station personnel have to wear these out on the hangar floor. We'll be providing you mission specific equipment at the next gate. The name's Gaz, by the way. I'm the United Globe liaison here at Amenitude. Now, Amenitude is technically a UG principality, but things get dicey with some colonial jurisdictions so I'll be your point of reference here. If you adjust your suit frequencies to the one displayed over the control tower, your mag-boots should lock at a strength close to Earth-G."

The Griffins typed out commands on their wrist displays, and after a moment, their boots each locked in place. Their feet now made magnetic clicking sounds every time they took a step on or off the ground with a muted electrical hum.

"Excellent," Gaz said, "Follow me." A traffic controller in a fluoro space suit with two red batons waved them through to the personnel lock, and then they proceeded to the colony's main terminal.

It was bustling inside the terminal, busier than any inter-orbital terminals on or around Earth. It was as wide as the hangar and far longer, with tiered levels ascending towards the colony proper side. The tiers had balconies overlooking the curved glass exterior, with a view over the pale grey surface of the Moon. Hundreds of people milled about, ferrying from one gate to the next as they moved between colonies or orbital stations, shopping at souvenir stalls and eating at cheap cafes and restaurants that offered a grand greyscale view of the little rock on which they found themselves.

Looking like some sort of military, the Griffins drew onlookers as they passed through. Some travellers even gawked. Paranormal events were rare and fringe enough that many still questioned their legitimacy, but they weren't so rare that the Griffin emblem would not draw the eye of a concerned citizen or two. Gaz ignored them as he ushered the Griffins onto one of the long travelators that led them to the far end of the terminal—a process taking several minutes. In the meantime, Bhanu gave Gaz access to the Griffin squad comms. He provided a briefing as they stood on the conveyor in rough double file.

As Gaz was introducing himself and the colony—the third largest colony on the Moon in terms of research and mining operations, but the second in terms of population—Aideen nudged up to Diondre and elbowed him.

"Hey," she said.

"What?"

"I'm sorry for calling you a pleb. Kieran said it hurt your feelings." She grinned mischievously. "I mean, I meant to hurt your feelings, but I didn't *mean* to hurt your feelings . . ."

Diondre smiled back, still stiff and uneasy. "If I couldn't take a little hazing, I never would have made it through college."

"Is Gaz boring you?" Bhanu turned and glared as the travelator trundled along past the nosey members of the public travelling in the opposite direction.

"No, ma'am," Aideen said, "just ensuring the squad's operational security."

Gaz cleared his throat. "As I was saying, there are a number of research facilities scattered around this colony base in particular. They can operate this close to a civilian population because the nature of the vacuum provides protection from most disasters."

"Only most?" Kieran asked.

Gaz shrugged. "Bureaucrats gonna bureaucrat."

"Figures," Kieran nodded.

"Now, for the classified part," Gaz said.

They reached the end of the travelator and Gaz ushered the team through a pressurised door into a much smaller hangar. It had an armoury and a rover sitting idly by a row of chairs for the squad.

"This will be your transport to Research Base Sigma. It went dark thirteen hours ago. Twelve and a half hours ago, one of the research scientists, Doctor Maragos, managed to squeeze off a distress signal. This signal included an encrypted data packet on the operations at Sigma so that the responding team wouldn't go in blind. I have been authorised by Global Response to share this information with you." As he was talking, he nodded to a group of Amenitude personnel who came in through a smaller pressure door. They started unloading equipment onto the display bench by the rover, "The research base was investigating lycanthropy . . ." the Griffins murmured among themselves, Kieran stiffened, his eyes hardening, ". . . they had six test subjects, all sourced from remote areas on Earth, captured humanely and brought up here to the secured research base for study. Their mission statement was to find a cure as well as a suppression serum for remote communities more likely to suffer from werewolf attacks. Somehow, one or more of the subjects broke loose and slaughtered the research staff."

He paused as the Griffins took this in.

"You motherfuckers," Kieran murmured, "You stupid motherfuckers!"

"Sergeant," Bhanu snapped, "Not now."

Kieran grumbled and quieted down. "Aye, Cap'n."

"He's got a point though, Ev," Aideen said, leaning in on her chair. "Firstly, this was done without Griffin involvement—Global Response founded us purely for this kind of stuff—so that's sus as fuck. And secondly, I mean, let's just go research lycanthropes on the fucking Moon! Every day cycle they'd be in full rage mode, permanently."

"I think that was the point of the research," Gaz said. "They exhausted all of their tests on human-form lycanthropes on Earth and it was too long between full Moons to research them properly in a transfigured state. This was deemed the safest option."

Kieran snorted.

"But you guys are trained to deal with this stuff, yeah? You call them mythos breaches? But really, shouldn't they be . . . I don't know, aren't werewolves talked about in folklore, not myths?"

"Some people say myths, some say fae, folk, or legends." Isao shrugged.

"It depends on where you're from," Solvi said.

"Or on how much of a nerd you are," Aideen chuckled.

"You need to stop arguing about this trivial shit," Kieran all but snarled. "We deal with paranormal threats. Call them what you will, fae, folktales, myths, monsters, but there's no need to split hairs over terminology. And yes, Gaz, we are trained to deal with them, but we aren't trained to deal with human stupidity!"

Bhanu shot him a glance, but turned back to Gaz. "You should have informed us of the nature of the threat before bringing us here. We have silver munitions back on the Hippogriff."

Gaz sighed. "So, brace yourselves for the bad news."

"Oh, that's good," Solvi muttered. "I thought this mission sounded easy enough."

"Preliminary scans show that sections of the base were vented during the incident. So we've provided these Lunar Government tactical EVA suits for you, as well as specialised silver weapons that operate like gas propelled harpoon guns. They should be able to work in the vacuum, although we only have six shots each."

Diondre pushed out of his chair and stalked over to the equipment. "No rear loading mechanisms. We'll have to reload from the barrel like muskets. And it seems the triggering mechanism takes a second to fire?"

"Yes," Gaz said, "It's the only way to fire in a vacuum with this tech; I'm sorry. The gasses need time to build up in the chamber to launch the projectile like a spear, and they can't be primed beforehand or it chances a misfire."

"Why do we even have a need to fire in the vacuum?" Isao cocked his ear towards Gaz as he spoke. "You know, where nothing can survive anyway?"

"Could have been sabotage," Solvi muttered. "Best be prepared for all outcomes."

"This is getting better and better," Aideen huffed.

"Why can't we take our own weapons?" Kieran asked. "We have vacuum capable firearms. Even if we didn't, once we seal Sigma Base we should be able to use them."

"Because the Lunar Government doesn't allow outside projectile weapons within any of the domes under their jurisdiction," Gaz answered. "This is the best we can do without causing an inter-orbital incident, and we aren't sure how the interior will hold up to small arms fire."

"Yeah, this mission is all kinds of messed up," Solvi said.

"Why do you even have these weapons?" Kieran asked.

"Sigma Base requisitioned them for extra security during some big experiment. They had to go through the red tape process and were due to be shipped right around the time the distress beacon was triggered," Gaz said.

"This seems like a really competent system you have up here," Kieran said. "Did they have any weapons at all?"

Gaz grimaced. "Non lethal silver pellet guns, and some classified suppression system."

"This is messed up," Aideen said.

"It doesn't matter," Bhanu snapped, "Griffins, we have our mission briefing and we know our parameters. Seek and destroy, retrieve data, and search and rescue. Gear up, wheels out in five!"

Part 4: Sigma Research Base

KIERAN AHMAD

It was as efficient a gear up as it could have been when you have six of the most highly trained soldiers in the world—well, *from* the world—putting on bulky vacuum capable gear they never trained with while listening to Gaz's rushed briefing on how to operate it.

The suits were made of a blue-grey synthetic material with armour plating resembling a bomb disposal squad's gear. They were reinforced at the joints with steel composite bands. The helmets were a three quarter dome with a reinforced rear plate, and the visors had an orange tint that could be adjusted to different levels of opacity from the wrist displays set into the gauntlets.

That kerfuffle took place half an hour ago. Now the Griffins were piled into the rover and traversing the rocky terrain of the Moon's surface. The sun shone, uninterrupted by atmosphere, and lit up the cratered, greyscale landscape brilliantly.

"I'm sure it looks lovely out there," Solvi grumbled, looking at the reinforced interior wall of the rover in front of her harness cradle. The rover bobbed along and her head bobbed with it inside the huge, domed helmet.

"You aren't paid to enjoy the scenery," Bhanu said.

"We aren't paid to use weapons we aren't trained with, either," Aideen said.

Bhanu rounded on her from the cockpit of the rover, but her expression was not stern. "I know, but it is what it is." She glanced at Kieran, who bobbed stoically in his harness.

Diondre was bringing up Sigma Base's specs; he looked up to notice the exchange, but remained silent.

"Diondre," Bhanu said, eyeing him. "Found anything useful?"

"Yes, ma'am. Sigma is a medium sized research base located within a crater twelve kilometres from Amenitude. Staff includes ten scientists, twelve subject security guards and a rotating roster of support staff, as well as the six *subjects* themselves. Recently the security was beefed up, something to do with a new experiment. Given that werewolves usually kill the victims instead of cursing them, and if they do curse them it takes at least a month for them to turn, I'd say the odds are even if all the subjects survived. Six v. six."

"It takes a month because that's when the next full Moon would be," Kieran said through gritted teeth. "The Moon may as well be always full during a day cycle up here. If the staff survived any wounds, well, let's just say that based off their numbers, we could expect twenty to thirty werewolves if our luck doesn't hold. And so far this situation reeks of bad luck."

"You all right, Kieran?" Diondre tried to follow Bhanu and Kieran's earlier advice and talk less formally. "You aren't your bubbly self."

The whole squad tensed. The rover suddenly felt more cramped than it already was. Kieran eyed Diondre for a while before answering. "About fifteen years ago now there was a disturbance near Wellington. There were quite a few casualties before the Griffins turned up."

"Werewolves?" Diondre asked.

Kieran nodded glumly.

"That must have been tough," Diondre said, "facing werewolves on your first mission. You must have been quite young."

"I was quite young—fourteen, and not yet a Griffin," Kieran said.

Diondre's brow furrowed. "I don't follow."

Aideen cut in. "This badass teenager kid wasn't the kind of person to sit around and wait for the werewolf to do its thing. He found some silverware in his neighbour's house—a bloody serving knife of all things—and went into the night and bullocked that bastard up himself."

"Whoa," Diondre said. "Remind me not to piss you off."

Kieran eyed him. "Then can we please not talk about it anymore? I lost family that night."

"Sure thing, Sergeant."

"If the history lesson is over," Isao said from the driving stick, "we just reached the lip of the crater Sigma Base is situated in. I've got a visual on the facility now."

"How's it look, Isao?" Bhanu asked.

"Not good, ma'am. The east side airlock is wide open."

"Roger that. Park the rover. We'll head down on foot. Lock and load, Griffins!"

The rover drifted to a halt; the interior depressurised with a hiss and a side panel opened to form a stairway onto the lunar surface. Besides their breath and the crackle of the comms in their ears, the only other sounds were the dull vibrations in the rover and the suits as the Griffins dinged into each other.

Aideen hopped out first, floating gracefully to the chalky ground and collapsing onto her face as the dust billowed up around her.

"Nice one, dickhead." Kieran went next and planted his feet squarely as he landed. He grabbed Aideen by the back of her suit and hauled her up. Within her helmet, a few red hairs fell from her cap and floated aimlessly around her face. "That must be annoying," Kieran sniffed, realising some stray strands of beard had floated up into his nostrils. "Fuck me."

"Deal with it, Griffins," Bhanu said, and hopped out next. "If you want to skirt presentation regulations, this is the penalty."

"It's a part of my culture!" Kieran protested.

"Yeah, mine too," Aideen laughed.

The Griffins disembarked without further incident and formed up on the rim of the crater, a slow decline of soft dust after a small drop off led to the research station below.

In essence, the facility was a large cluster of white and grey corridors welded together in an airtight network. On the far western side was a large square complex looming out of the maze of tunnels—that was the lab. It looked much like a warehouse from this distance, but with a darkened skylight set into its top. To the north side of the interlocking tunnels was a two storied hexagonal structure made entirely of steel, just as large as the lab, and lined with square windows with semi closed black shutters. The south side sported a large habitation dome that bulged out of the facility like a cyst. Within it were a dozen three levelled boxlike apartment towers. Even from this distance, the Griffins could make out the greenery between the units.

On the eastern side, the side that the Griffins looked on from, there was a small depot. It had a single rover docked next to a maintenance control room with an observation screen. Near the dock was an open airlock. The ground in front of the opening was gouged and streaked with red—as the air exploded out, it must have dragged some viscera with it too. Within the opening, the amber alarm light strobed constantly, lighting the darkness like an ominous beacon.

"Well," Bhanu's voice crackled over the comms, "that's our entry point. Griffins, let's fly." She hopped off the rim and down into the soft dust of the crater wall, half jumping, half falling on her way towards the dead base.

The other Griffins leaped after her, but before following, Kieran took one last look across the moonscape. The lunar colony was lit up on the horizon, the only other sign of humanity in this forsaken place. The Earth hung suspended in the night sky beyond it, a shining blue light about to dip from sight.

East, Kieran noted, realising the rim of the crater must have bordered on the far side of the Moon from the Earth. *When in doubt, look to the east.* He tapped his leg, where beneath the space suit his gyroscope was stored. He finally took a deep breath, and jumped into the crater.

It was only a ten minute journey of comical ambulation down the soft dusty surface of the crater interior. The Griffins reached a point where the crater flattened out and they made for the silent, strobing maw into the station. They passed over the mangled, desiccated body of a man; his face was locked rigid in anguish. It was not clear whether he died from being mauled or due to exposure to the vacuum. The Griffins moved past the body and towards the opening.

"Why don't we try an airlock cycle breach?" Isao asked.

"Stupid to suggest it, seeing as the airlock is clearly open," Bhanu said. "And even if it wasn't, we have no idea how fragile the station is, nor do we want to advertise our presence. Solvi, take point."

Solvi pushed past Isao and reached the opening first, pressing her form—bulky due to the space suit—against the side of the door and aiming down the corridor with her silver spear. The long weapon would have been unwieldy in Earth-G. The barrel was as long as she was tall, and it was weighted at the butt with gas canisters and firing mechanisms. She scanned the hallway and found nothing through the amber strobing light but blood caked to the walls, floors, and ceiling.

Besides the signs of a massacre, the place looked like any other mass produced vacuum safe facility. It had practical grey and white steel panelling which would usually be lit with standard white fluorescents, but with the alarm triggered it was painted with strobing amber light.

She motioned with her hand and Isao and Aideen filtered in next, followed by Bhanu, Kieran, and Diondre. Solvi entered after them.

"Engage mag boots," Bhanu ordered.

The floor reverberated in the silence as six pairs of boots locked onto Sigma's floor.

"How's atmo looking, Isao?" Bhanu asked.

Isao was kneeling at a panel inside the airlock. "Majority of the interior seems to be free of breaches. But I can't operate anything through this terminal without a command key."

Bhanu produced a data port from one of her suit's pouches and gave it to Isao. He inserted it into a socket by the panel and typed away on his wrist pad. The airlock slid shut and the hallway hissed as he flooded the compartment with atmosphere. The silence of the vacuum was broken by the deafening rush of air and the blaring alarm in tandem with its strobing light.

"Isao!" Bhanu ordered.

"Yeah, yeah, give me a moment." He typed a few more commands onto his wrist pad, and then switched to typing on the airlock panel keyboard and the alarm finally stopped. The Griffins were left in darkness, save for the emergency floor lighting directing them towards the evacuation route which would take them to the rover dock.

"We gonna get lights?" Diondre asked.

"Sigma is low on power; it's operating life support and emergency functions only," Isao said.

"Switch on shoulder and weapon mounted lights," Bhanu ordered, but the Griffins were already doing so before she finished speaking. "And let's get this door open." She marched to the end of the sealed corridor.

The Griffins congregated around the door at the far end of the airlock and trained their weapons on it.

"Keep in mind, we can expect anywhere between six . . ." she glanced at Kieran, ". . . to thirty hostiles in here. There's no telling how many of the station's staff survived, or what state the data we need to retrieve may be in. We don't really know what to expect, so eyes up. Diondre, take point, Isao, breach on my mark . . . mark!"

The door slid open and a furry creature leaped out at them, bypassing Diondre and tackling Kieran to the ground.

"Hold fire!" Kieran bellowed as the creature slobbered over his visor. "It's just a dog!"

"Greetings!" it said in a monotone, digital voice as its tail wagged. "I am designated Floof!"

"It's got one of those neural translators." Solvi said as the rest of the Griffins moved through the breach to secure the four way corridor junction on the other side.

"Focus, Solvi."

"Easy up, Ev. If the werewolves were in the immediate area, they would have torn Floof apart," Aideen said as she reached down and toggled a switch on the dog's collar.

Floof's voice changed to a cutesy speech pattern. "It's heckin scary in there!" he said. "There are toothy boys causing all kinds of ruckus!"

"I'm sure they are! You've been a good boy!" Aideen petted Floof as best she could through her bulky gloves.

"The goodest boy!" Floof wagged his tail.

"Ev," Solvi said, "More bodies in the adjacent corridors. Not our hostiles, but it's their handiwork."

"Roger, Aideen. Kieran, lock that shit down and move in."

"Are you here to help my fren?" Floof asked, sidling up to Aideen as they moved into the junction.

"Is your friend still alive?" Kieran asked.

"Yes! She's my bestest fren . . . since the others met the toothy boys that is." His tail stopped wagging.

"Grim," Aideen said.

The Griffins fluidly spread out into the three connecting corridors to create a perimeter. Kieran and Aideen took positions in the central corridor, Diondre and Bhanu covered the corridor on the right, and Solvi and Isao spilled into the left. Floof kept close to Aideen's leg.

"It's very scary in here!" Floof said.

"I know, buddy," Aideen said as she tousled between his ears. "I'll keep you safe."

The doors connecting each tunnel to the junction slammed closed.

"Fuck, Isao, what the hell are you doing?" Kieran slammed his shoulder into the door.

"I didn't do shit. Someone else is overriding the system."

"Isao," Bhanu's voice grew stern. "Your job was to have control of the system."

"I'm trying, Ev. Someone's locked me out. The master key isn't even responding."

"So this must have been sabotage then? And the saboteur is still here," Kieran commented. He eyed Floof, "Where is your friend, little one?"

Floof barked in response, "somewhere."

"Right, right, give me a second." From her corridor, Bhanu pulled up a schematic on her wrist pad and formulated a plan. "All right, all right . . . seeing as we're all separated . . . Diondre and I will head through to the maintenance control room and try to override whoever is in the system. Then we'll sweep through the habitation dome. Isao, Solvi, your corridor leads to the containment block; do a sweep but be careful. Hopefully by then I have the doors open to the lab and you can link up with Kieran and Aideen. As for Kieran and Aideen, the lab is down the end of your corridor. Secure any research data you can, link up with Isao and Solvi, and sweep the remaining corridors on your way to the habitation dome. We should meet somewhere between habitation and the lab. Acknowledge?"

"Roger that," Solvi said.

"Aideen here, Kieran and I are moving down the corridor now."

"Right," Bhanu responded. "Let's un-fuck this situation, Griffins."

Part 5: Divided

ISAO SAITO

Isao stacked up against the half closed pressure door and motioned for Solvi to join him. An electric sign above read *'containment,'* but it dulled as its power waned. Isao took a deep breath and grounded himself—a technique that lost its edge on a magnetised floor in lunar-G. When he was ready, he gave Solvi a nod, gripped the half closed door, and heaved it open with groaning clamour. Solvi stepped into the opening and swept the dim interior with her weapon.

"How's it look in there?" Isao asked.

"Spooky." She made a hand gesture and the two entered the cell block with a sweeping search pattern.

The room was a cell block of sorts housed within the hexagonal containment structure. It was two stories tall, with high windows on one side letting the pale silvery light filter down into the large, gloomy interior. There were reinforced glass cells, or holding pens, set into the walls on the outer side. Each cell was large, like a horse's stable, but contained a small cot with a sink and toilet, as well as a large mat in the centre, of which most were chewed up and torn to shreds. The outer wall of the cells had windows with half closed emergency shutters looking out over the bleak landscape.

The most concerning thing about the cells was that all of them were open.

"They can jettison these cells," Solvi realised, inspecting the control panel next to the closest cell. "Maybe a failsafe measure?"

"Not a very good one if they didn't use it." Isao twitched as a wall panel down the cell block sparked, illuminating the space with a bright light for only an instant. "This stinks."

"You can only smell what's inside your suit; you should have showered this morning."

"Come on, don't joke around. There's a control centre down this way, at the end of the wing, and some big cages on some kind of tracks."

"Must be for transporting them to the lab," Solvi theorised. "Let's move up."

The two made their way down the cell block, checking each empty cell as they went. At the end there was a corner and presumably another cell block to search once they rounded it. The control centre was a large, windowed room set into the far side from the corner with inert monitors and control systems inside.

The windows were covered in blood, and there were several slumped shapes inside.

Isao made to cross the floor to the control centre when Solvi hissed at him. She tapped the side of her helmet and Isao recognised it as a signal to listen. He pressed against the wall by the corner and strained his ears. His hearing hadn't been the same since the run in with the Fujin sprite. Usually he had to listen over an incessant ringing in his ears, and he was glad of Solvi's help. But now that he was focused, he could hear it.

Something was around the corner. Whatever it was, it was big, with a heaving, rasping breath.

A shiver travelled down Isao's spine, and he readied his weapon.

Steeling himself, Isao rounded the corner and trained his weapon on the largest centre of mass he could find in the gloom. His training as a counter-paranormal operative filtered out the initial shock and revulsion of the pile of dismembered bodies that the hulking beast was perched upon. Its snout was ravenously digging through the splintered open chest of a poor sanitation worker. The lifeless eyes of the janitor stared back at Isao as his head lolled around with every nip and tear of his innards, each jolt accompanied by a wet crunch and snap.

Isao breathed deep, and squeezed the trigger.

The weapon clicked. Nothing happened. The beast—the wolf man—looked up from its feast and snarled with bloody fangs. Yellow eyes reflected the dim light of the Moon that poured through the windows. They fixated on the Griffin with hyper focus.

Isao gasped. He squeezed the trigger again. Another click—another nothing.

The werewolf snarled and discarded its current meal, keen to peel the flesh from prey still wriggling. It was a huge, bulky creature, standing a head taller than Isao—and that was with it hunched low to leer at him. It had a shaggy mess of wet grey and black fur, its torso and shoulders were large enough to rival a bull, and it had a narrowing waist with long, muscular legs.

It hunched low to crawl over the mound of bodies on its enormous forelegs, reaching out with large clawed hands to pull itself forward. Each click of black claw on steel tile indicated another arm's length travelled between it and its next meal—Isao.

Sweat poured down Isao's brow and stung his eyes as he stumbled back. The werewolf pounced with a roar to claim its prize. Isao brought the silver spear up like a bar and its jaws clamped around it, rending metal and knocking him onto the ground with its bulk pressing down on top of him. While wrestling with the weapon in its mouth, it tore with claws at Isao's reinforced suit. Isao tried to wrench the weapon free, to nick at the werewolf with the exposed silver tip, but he was fighting a losing battle.

Something hissed and whistled—the werewolf yelped and lifted off Isao a second after pouncing on him, tumbling across the floor with a long, silver spear skewering straight through its abdomen. Solvi slid next to Isao on her knees while drawing another spear from the makeshift quiver at her side to slot into the barrel of the weapon. She kept her sight on the werewolf as it writhed and whined, shrivelling into the naked form of a dead man.

"You have to hold the trigger down until the gasses build up, moron," she gasped. "You never listen to briefings!"

"I listen to weapons briefings!" Isao retorted, pulling himself up and inspecting his weapon. "I just tune out during the formal warnings. Goddamn it." Isao twisted a knob by one of the gas cylinders until it hissed and the pressure gauge registered an increase. "Fucking things are awfully put together; Lunans couldn't maintain a BB gun."

"You sure you didn't just knock that while bumbling around?" Solvi clicked the new spear into place.

"Whatever!" Isao shoved her back and crawled over to the werewolf with his silver spear in hand. He kept an eye down the adjacent cell block, looking for movement amongst the bodies, the bloodied cells, or the gantries that lined the ceiling. He rolled the body over. "Black male, mid-fifties. One down, five to go."

"No, not five to go. That man doesn't match the description of the test subjects. We're outnumbered here."

"Fuck," Isao muttered, "Fuck!" He stalked over to the control centre window, "Well these ones all committed suicide."

Solvi was by his side a moment later, all chiding gone from her voice. "Wouldn't you do the same?"

Isao sighed. "I don't know."

A growl rattled them from their discussion and they spun to aim down the body strewn cell block to find . . . nothing. Isao made eye contact with Solvi, and they both nodded to each other, noting each other's fearful expressions. Isao took comfort in the shared fact. Even though their muscles felt frozen in place, even though their hairs stood on end beneath their suits, they started their sweep down the next cell block, ready for imminent attack.

BHANU EVERLY

"Moving up on maintenance control room now," Bhanu said, tapping her comms, "How's the rest of the team looking?"

A burst of static was her only reply. She tried to fight the worry for her squad from building in her chest.

"This is composite steel panelling, ma'am," Diondre told her, slapping the walls with the palm of his hand. "I doubt any external signals will transmit until we hook the squad's comms into Sigma's system."

"Can we do that through maintenance control?"

"Theoretically."

"Then let's move."

They rounded a corner and found the crumpled-in remains of a pressurised door and a palely lit room beyond it.

Bhanu and Diondre moved up the hallway swiftly and stacked up on either side of the door. *What I wouldn't give for some kind of flash grenade, bloody lunatics.* She smirked. She realised Diondre was eyeing her, so she set her face sternly and gave a nod. The two swept their weapons from the floor to shoulder height—on account of the length of the unruly weapons—as they breached the maintenance room.

It was in a state—full of strewn janitorial and maintenance equipment as well as wrecked consoles. The pale light reflecting off the Moon's surface shone into the room through the observation screen that looked out to the docked rover. The primary screen itself was cracked open, a secondary barrier with large warning labels printed over it had slammed down in place as a countermeasure for atmospheric leaks. The place was littered with clumps of damp fur, claw marks, and the odd blood spatter.

Among it all, one console flickered dimly.

"Clear," Diondre said. "That observation screen . . . it looks like it was broken from the outside."

"That's not possible, Diondre. Check that console." Bhanu turned to cover the entrance while he went to work.

Diondre slung his weapon over his shoulder and tapped on the computer keys slowly with his bulky gloves. "System's barely functioning. I can restore some power to get the lights on and have better working doors. But it'll take a few minutes for the emergency generators to reroute."

"Do it. What about comms?"

Diondre replied with muttered profanities as he struggled to work the keyboard. "Someone with admin access is blocking me from patching us in. I have one active transponder, though, somewhere in the habitation dome. Doctor Maragos."

"Do the werewolves have trackers?" Bhanu asked. She waited as Diondre navigated the system.

Diondre tensed before he answered, his voice tightening. "None that I can find. It's possible their transformation blocks them."

How would he know that? Bhanu cocked her head. "How do you figure, Diondre?"

"I have a bead on several dead transponders throughout the base, but there aren't enough to account for the amount of staff on site. So I'm guessing the difference is made up from transformed people. There are definitely werewolves roaming the base."

"Fuck."

Bhanu took stock of the situation. The Griffins were very likely outnumbered and split up, and they had no real control of the system.

"The only person who can be keeping us out of the system is that scientist. You said she was in the habitation dome?"

"Yes, ma'am."

"All right then, that's our next stop. Move out, Griffin."

As they readied to leave, the flicking console blinked with text, an unanswered prompt from Sigma's system. It read:

'Allow G.R. - F.I.N. comms access to Sigma?
... Y/N ...'

But Bhanu did not notice the prompt as she led Diondre out of the room.

KIERAN AHMAD

Kieran's muscles tensed, as heavy as lead as he pressed against the corridor wall, straining to listen for signs of movement through the open laboratory doors. But he heard nothing save for the incessant patter of Floof's wagging tail beating against his leg.

"As much as I like this dog, it is far from practical to have around," he said.

"Well, as we mentioned before," Aideen commented, looking up from her weapon's sights, "if Floof isn't reacting, then there mustn't be anything in there."

"I'm not so convinced. Floof, anything through these doors?"

"I'd love to help, fren! But this place is swimming in smells!" his tongue lolled from his mouth. "But if I see any toothy boys, I'll bork at them! It doesn't scare them off, and they always bork back. But now you're here to bork with me!"

"You know, that didn't fill me with any confidence at all," Kieran said.

"Had you any to begin with?" Aideen asked. She shuffled down the hallway to the door and peered inside.

"You know, I guess I didn't," Kieran laughed, "You ready?"

"Ready," Aideen answered.

Kieran bolted through the door with a yell and swept the area with his light. The theory behind this approach being any werewolves would have sensed them approaching by now. But by running in like a madman it might distract them enough to at least get a shot off before being torn limb from limb.

Sadly, Kieran found himself yelling at an empty room.

"Well," he said, waving Aideen in as his shoulders sagged, "it felt good to let out that pent up angst at least. Bruh, this place is trashed."

The lab was a large square room, matching the bulky warehouse appearance it had from the outside. It was dim, like the rest of the base so far, with flickering monitors and trashed scientific equipment strewn about the place. There was a large roller door on one side leading off to the cell blocks with tracks for individual cells to be transported on. In the middle of the room was a huge glass cell—shattered to bits—with a medical cot within, sporting broken restraints. There was a large skylight above the cell, which offered a window to the black void above, spackled with starlight. As with the entrance hallway, there was coagulated blood splattered over most of the surfaces.

"This terminal is slightly less smashed than the rest."

Aideen gestured to a humming computer. She inserted a hard drive into the machine and started typing away at the keypads.

"God damn it, these gloves are bulky. But hey! I've got a whole lot of logs here—audio files too."

"Any recording during the incident?" Kieran asked.

"I'll play the last one while we have a looksee around." Aideen typed in the command and the two Griffins swept through the lab, pillaging data drives and shoving them into their oversized suit pouches as they went.

The recording was garbled in some places, but intelligible enough for the Griffins to comprehend as they searched. "Doctor Maragos, research log, fifteenth of July, twenty-one fourteen. Our last test on subject four, Roger Smith, was successful. The serum appeared to reduce the more extreme carnal drives to hunt and we could form some rudimentary communications. Initial experiments showed that Subject Four would still feed on us within seconds given the chance. This insight was derived by comparing the subject's transformed brain waves to his untransformed state both before and after the serum was introduced.

"While Four is still aggressive, we are one step closer to perhaps having a biological weapon for fringe communities if they ever suffer from Lycanthropic intrusions. It even reduces the time transformed after full Moon exposure from an average of twelve hours to an almost instantaneous reversion. Some factors seem to influence this such as exhaustion levels and meal frequency, but it is promising.

"We are still unsure what causes the transformation process. But the leading theory is that Moon rock has some property that, when reflecting ultraviolet light, triggers the lycanthrope curse in a subject's visual nerve. If we block their view of the Moon, transformation is halted, but experiments show that when possible they are always compelled to try and look even at detriment to themselves. Subject Three even broke her own arm to free her restraints and tear her blindfold off.

"We need to see after Four transforms back if he still has this compulsion after being injected with the serum. Unfortunately, this is still a curse we are dealing with. We may struggle and make ways to understand how it manifests in our world, but the paranormal nature means we may never have a full understanding through our current means alone."

There was some muttering as Doctor Maragos spoke to a fellow scientist in the background of the recording, and then she went back to narrating her log.

"Yes, despite this gap in knowledge there is still a push from our bankrollers to try and apply this to controlling Four while in a transfigured state. So far our contract has managed to keep that line of thought at bay. Our priority has always been to cure lycanthropy outright. But from a purely hypothetical viewpoint, the idea is as probable as it is intriguing.

"It was always assumed that lycans were rogue hunters. But this is just an unfortunate—or fortunate, depending on who you ask—side effect of how one is usually cursed. Usually these people isolate themselves after surviving an encounter with such a beast, not wishing to cause undue harm. The rare accounts of lycanthropes encountering each other coincidentally have ended in bloodshed. But that's not the case when more than two are assembled together for a long duration of time. Now that we have gathered them, corralled them unwillingly into a small space, they have formed pack behaviour, loyal to those they consider their own. While transformed, the lycans do not respond well when their kin are taken, or experimented on in front of each other. There is teamwork—a sense of family, even. This might be a means of control down the line, but it is not our focus right now.

"It is truly remarkable how little we know of this affliction, but Serum 3-H is our first successful foray into getting a handle on it. We . . ."

"Aideen, contact!" Kieran yelled over the recording as he trained his light on a huddled figure in the corner. "Identify yourself, now!"

"P-p-please don't hurt me." He was a naked man in his mid forties, wedged between two tables.

"Identify yourself, now!"

"B-Barry, s-s-s-station security."

"You've done a shit job here, Barry," Aideen said, moving around Kieran and training her weapon on Barry.

Kieran gave her a look and she shrugged. "Why are you naked?" he asked.

"I've been bitten," Barry held out a trembling limb and Floof growled, shrinking back.

"All right, all right, all right," Kieran breathed. "Why aren't you trying to maul us right now?"

"Station power failed some point between the breach and now, m-m-m-mirror lowered from skylight." He pointed up, still shaking, "I woke up in the dark a few hours ago. Please, you have to help me! There's a serum, they were working on a serum."

"Easy there, easy." Kieran shouldered his weapon and crouched down in front of the terrified man. "By the sounds of it the serum wasn't quite done yet; do you know where it is?"

"S-s-s-s-s . . ."

"Breathe, brother, breathe."

Barry took a moment to control his breathing, "S-secure vault between here and habitation. Doors are sealed. No power." He pointed weakly at the skylight again.

"Do you know how the breach happened?" Aideen swept the area briefly before looking back at the man.

"No, yes. Someone hacked . . . my head hurts . . . someone must have hacked into cell control, opened all the pens while the subjects were transformed for a group experiment. The scientists wanted to see how they worked as a team. It was that bitch Helena's idea."

"She's my fren!" Floof barked happily.

"That dog's alive? They never seemed to take notice of it." Barry coughed. "Our suppression systems didn't respond properly. Due to our regulations," he coughed again, "we couldn't be armed unless in the same room as a test subject, everyone with a weapon was in that room when they got out, all they had were pellet guns, didn't even have our new lethal weapons. We were overwhelmed in seconds. If the suppression systems were disabled, my other officers were likely locked out from the armoury by the secure vault. Do you have any pain killers?"

"Yeah, ease up, brother." Kieran reached for the medical pouch on his leg. "Aideen, figure out how to get those doors open without power. We need that serum."

"Aye." Aideen scanned the far wall, "What about Isao and Solvi?"

"Shit, Barry, can we get into the cell blocks without power?"

Barry's eyes widened. "What? That's where their den is! Some are still transformed. I heard them howling a few moments ago."

"Fuck! Isao, Solvi!" Kieran barked into his comms. "There's just static."

"We need power," Aideen said. The station rumbled, and then started humming. "Oh hey, Cap'n must have gotten the power up!"

Lights started flickering to bright fluorescence, highlighting the blood.

"Oh no." Barry retreated into his nook.

"Don't worry brother, we aren't gonna open any doors before we're ready. Nothing's getting in here," Kieran said, trying to reassure him.

"They already are in here," he exclaimed, and held up his arm. "Mirror!"

Kieran looked up through the skylight as a large mirror lowered down into place, reflecting light from the Moon's surface into the laboratory. "Well, fuck me." The brightening lab was flooded in silver light. He shuffled back and trained his weapon on Barry, whose voice grew hoarse and skin grew taut. "Aideen! Get over here, NOW!"

Barry twisted, snapped and whined like a stuck pig, writhing on the clinical white tiles of the lab. The whites of his eyes turned dull and blood shot, his lips pulled back from his gums, revealing black veins and horridly sharpening teeth. His fingernails split through his skin, growing into wicked curled black claws, and his skin stretched and tore as the rippling muscles and shaggy fur sprouted through it.

He was growing.

Kieran lamented, the horrible memories from his encounter as a teenager came flooding back with a wave of adrenaline.

Aideen leaped onto one of the tables and dashed across them to the far side of the room, trying to get a good shot at the mirror that was funnelling the deadly moonlight into the space.

"It's no use," Kieran said solemnly, training his weapon on the changing, twisting, snapping mass, "The transformation's started."

He squeezed the trigger. It hissed as the gasses siphoned into the firing chamber, and then whistled as the spear released and impaled the poor man.

Barry stopped writhing with a yelp, and his shifting form reverted to that of a dead, naked human with a terrified expression.

"You did the right thing, Kieran."

"I know." Kieran pulled another spear from the quiver at his back and went about reloading the clumsy weapon.

Floof growled, "Toothy boys."

The corrugated roller door behind Aideen shifted, the one with the corridor leading to the cell block. A vicious howling echoed through the reverberating steel as it started inching upwards.

"Whelp, that's either Isao and Solvi having another row, or . . ." Aideen trained her weapon on the opening roller door.

It ripped open at the bottom like tissue paper as a pack of werewolves poured from the gaping hole.

Aideen swore and fell back from the table, landing on her arse as the first vicious claw swiped the empty space where she had been an instant beforehand. Her fall was muted in the lunar gravity, but her magnetic boots slammed down faster than the rest of her body, which was disorienting. Still, it was not disorienting enough to hinder her reflexes. She brought up her weapon and squeezed the trigger as the first werewolf leered over the table, snarling with a lapping, salivating tongue. She tracked its head as the gasses built up in the weapon and let loose. The spear skewered the beast between the eyes and propelled the transfiguring corpse backwards with enough force to pierce through the still opening roller door. As it trundled upwards the limp, impaled body of a now human woman was hoisted up with it.

Aideen struggled off her arse up into a crouch and dove to slide under the next table. Her mag boots halted her slide short. They dragged her to a stop and the pack descended on her ravenously, flipping the table which careened off surreally in slow motion and they clawed at her from every angle. She brought up her empty weapon to stave them off as their vicious mauling and slashing glanced off her suit's protection, for now. It was only a matter of time before one claw slipped through the gap in the armour plating, or until one werewolf decided to clamp its jaws around the domed space helmet.

Floof charged in and bit one of the creature's ankles, a pitiful David against a mighty Goliath. It roared and turned to swipe at Floof, but upon seeing the dog it stopped short and gently shoved it away.

Kieran watched helplessly from the far side of the lab, fumbling to reload the silver spear. It was not nerves that made him fumble, nor panic or a lack of understanding of the weapon. It was the realisation that he would not reload and fire in time to save Aideen—that even if he could, he could only take out one werewolf, and would need to start the whole clumsy process all over again.

Standing there, holding the spear in one hand, the gun in the other, he was brought back to Wellington, all those years ago. He was just a teenager with a silver knife; there was a hulking beast at the end of the darkened street, prowling for his sister after it had feasted on his brother.

That's what always confused Kieran about Griffin Command. Once they recruited him after that incident, they were always so careful not to send him to any potential wolf sights, for fear of a regression to that traumatic night. They were worried that the experience would break him, grip him with terror. It confused him, because even though he was a small, untrained kid back then, even though the terror gripped his heart and squeezed as it did right now, he still did what needed to be done.

Griffin Command was right. He had reverted back to that boy. But the thing was, back then when it came to protecting his own, he didn't give a fuck about the terror, and he sure as shit didn't give a fuck about the terror now.

He discarded the spear gun, and held the spear itself in both hands, letting out a beastly, guttural roar. He stomped his feet and slammed the haft of the spear into his chest like the traditions of his countrymen.

It was so fierce that even through his helmet the roar caused the pack of werewolves to pause in their frenzy and consider him. Even Aideen—on her back and surrounded by nightmare beasts—craned her neck to see what monster could roar like that, and she saw a Griffin.

Kieran charged into the midst of the werewolves with a fury, whipping the spear around to slash eyes, stab at sides and slam into jaws. There were four of the beasts and two flinched back as one was skewered through the head with a wet, sizzling crack. Kieran ripped the spear from the shrivelling corpse with a *schlick* as one of the werewolves slammed into him from the rear. It was twice his mass, maybe, but Kieran was beyond caring about such trivial things. He planted his feet and pivoted, throwing the bulk of the beast around him—aided by the lunar-G—and stabbed it through the shoulder.

Its flesh seared and it snarled, retreating from the wounding blow and taking the embedded spear along with it.

Kieran fumbled to grab a replacement spear from his quiver, but the other two werewolves had regained their frenzy and rushed to tear him apart.

Seeing the danger, Kieran abandoned the bulky process of reaching around his suit and decided on the unexpected. He moved to meet the werewolves with nothing but his clenched fists. He clobbered the first one in the jaw and it flinched back—more surprised than hurt. Kieran followed up by kicking at its hunched face and punching it again and again. He manoeuvred around the beast as he struck to keep it between him and the other werewolf as it attempted to rush him.

Kieran was not fooled by macho rage. He knew he could not beat the werewolf in a contest of brawn. But he knew he could beat it in a contest of will. If he simply *acted* as if he could tear it apart, maybe—just maybe—its instincts would kick into gear and it would believe the threat was genuine.

So Kieran moved in with a roar, wrapping his arms around the bulging werewolf's neck and wringing with all his might. It howled in terror and tried to shake him off, but his will proved the greater.

Its companion circled around to tear him off, but Aideen had reloaded. She squeezed off a shot and it pierced through its bowels. The spear flew through its body, trailing burning entrails through its back as it let out its terrible death knell and collapsed in a writhing, shrivelling heap.

Aideen pulled out another spear and charged into the wrestling match between wolf man and beast man. Kieran pummelled his opponent in the eye as he held on for dear life and Aideen yelled as she skewered her spear through its chest.

It whimpered and collapsed, shrivelling into another poor human corpse as the two Griffins righted themselves to face down the final, wounded werewolf.

It snarled, using its teeth to wrench the spear from its shoulder with a howl, and bolted for the roller doors.

Aideen moved to hit the close button, lest any reinforcements came through, as Kieran planted himself in the doorway, howling and yelling at the retreating beast in victory.

"You do not mess with *my* pack, little pup! You do not mess with my pack!"

The door groaned shut, the torn section at the bottom sagged unevenly against the ground and the pinned corpse sagged with it. Once the door crinkled closed to a halt, Aideen collapsed by the panel, panting.

"Are you hurt? Did they get through your suit?" Kieran rasped as he stumbled over to her, flinching as Floof bolted past him to attend to her as well.

"I'm . . ." Aideen checked her marred suit. "My suit isn't breached. I'm in one piece, but only barely," she said, and looked at him. "What the fuck was that?"

"I told you, I took up Pilates." Kieran collapsed next to her and let out a deep, rasping laugh.

She chuckled with him. "I always knew you were a housewife," she said, and batted him on the shoulder. "Thanks."

"You would have done the same for me."

"No the fuck I wouldn't have!"

Floof barked. "Toothy boys are helping their frens down there."

"Shit," Aideen cursed, keying her comms. "We need to warn Isao and Solvi. Fuck—still just static. What do we do? Cell block, or habitation to regroup with Bhanu and Diondre?"

"That's a good question," Kieran said.

The station rumbled, and a computerised voice issued a warning over the speakers. "Please be advised, pressurisation breach in cell blocks. Avoid the area."

"Well, either they're sitting pretty in the vacuum surrounded by suffocating werewolves, or . . ." Aideen trailed off, not wanting to finish the thought. "We should get that serum, link up with the Cap'n, and then see what we can do to help Isao and Solvi from a position of strength."

Kieran mumbled something in Arabic.

"What was that?" Aideen asked. She hefted herself up and then helped Kieran to his feet.

"A prayer for our team."

He started collecting the spears from the dead.

Part 6: Conquered

SOLVI HAGEN

The spear launched from the gun and pierced the leaping werewolf mid flight. As terrible and fast as it was in the lighter gravity, Solvi still managed to hit it. It snapped back with a yelp and collapsed into its pack mates.

"They just keep coming!"

Solvi desperately reached for another spear. As she reloaded a werewolf leaped from the gantry above and slammed into Isao, knocking him to the ground and pinning him in place.

"Isao!"

Solvi rushed to help, but the werewolf had already torn off Isao's pauldron and sunk its teeth through his suit and into his flesh.

The inside of his helmet was sprayed with coughed blood. The teeth must have sunk very deep indeed. She raised her weapon to fire, but his pleading voice from under the werewolf stopped her.

"Just get in the cell!"

She didn't have time to argue as more of the beasts rushed in. She ran and leaped into the closest cell while holding down the trigger on her weapon. She spun as she leaped and fired a round through the creature that was mauling her teammate.

It recoiled from him with a yelp as the spear pierced its chest. She fumbled to reload as Isao dragged himself to his feet and stumbled over, dreadfully slow compared to the wave of fur and muscle and teeth that was rolling towards him.

She slammed her penultimate spear into the gun and raised it to cover him. He reached the cell and hit the door control, but then he halted in place as the door slid shut between them.

A sudden dread tore through Solvi like a cold weight dropped through her guts as she realised what he had done.

"What the fuck are you doing?" she demanded, racing forward to batter through the door. But it was designed to keep werewolves at bay, and she was just a puny human.

"I'm bitten," he keyed the jettison sequence of the cell, and held his spear gun in place to jam the secondary pair of pressure doors that closed over the first set.

"Isao, don't do this; your suit is compromised!"

The pressure doors clenched shut around his spear gun—they bent it with their hydraulic strength, but remained open.

The clamps in place behind Solvi's cell hissed as they released, and the jettison warning sounded, a droning beat increasing in speed and pitch the closer she came to imminent expulsion.

"It's okay!" Isao grunted as a werewolf slammed him from behind.

The whole pack descended upon him against the cell and his pained, bloodied face was pinned to the glass doors as they did their vicious work. A flood of tears threatened to break Solvi into a spluttering mess, but they never came as she watched helplessly with her hands pressed against the transparent surface. The tears were held back by the panic and horror of her comrade's demise. They tore through his suit and flesh as she waited for the room to void, and for him to be granted release from pain.

The cell was jettisoned with a rush of force. Solvi was thrown from her feet as the compartment launched from the cell block like a torpedo. Isao's spear gun that propped the pressure doors open was torn from its place to follow her, along with the doors themselves, Isao's dismembered corpse, and the frenzied pack of werewolves that had been attacking them.

Solvi slammed into the far side of the cell as its trajectory sent it ricocheting off the wall of the crater and up the rise. It tumbled end over end and threw her around inside like a rag doll.

The air escaped from the cell through vents, air holes of a kind for when the cell was safely inside—decompression holes now that it had vented. Thankfully, her suit kept its integrity, even as her visor cracked, and even as her wrist readout flashed red with warning signs every time she slammed into another wall of the cell.

She wasn't sure how much time had passed when she groaned and pushed herself up. Her nose and mouth were bleeding, dripping onto the inside of her cracked visor. Her bones and organs ached, but she was alive. She looked around to gain her bearings. The cell was embedded somewhere halfway up the crater's side, its walls were cracked open, and the trail of the rampaging compartment was marked by deep gouges in the Moon's surface.

She blinked through pain bleared eyes and followed the trail back to Sigma Base, registering Isao's mangled corpse, the hole in the cell block, and—to her addled horror—the pack of werewolves picking themselves up about the clouds of Moon dust that kicked up in their frenzy.

They gathered upon the bleak grey surface. Saliva and blood were drawn out of the mouths, nose and eyes like jets of mist, and sweat steamed out of their glands. All moisture was forcibly pulled out from them by the nature of the vacuum. But they were alive, and enraged at their current torment.

Solvi cried out in terror as they sighted her cell up the rise, and started bounding towards it.

Her hands were shaking, her mind was racing with the impossibility of it all—but her training kicked in. These were cursed beings. What was possible to the human mind had nothing to do with what was happening in front of her; she had to force herself to accept it.

She centred herself, and decided to act.

She took a quick inventory—disregarding the building panic that rose in her chest like hot, bubbling mud, clinging to her lungs and stifling her breath. She had one spear left in her gun—the last in her quiver had cracked in half. She held the snapped spearhead close like a pathetic little knife and fired her gun at the cracked glass wall of the cell. It exploded outwards in a shower of slowly spinning shards and she crawled out of the larger opening. Stumbling to her feet, she bounded up the crater, making for her only hope of escape—the rover they had parked on the rim.

The werewolves bounded up the slope after her, every leap and jump sending them further than she could hope to carry herself. They would soon catch up; it would be close.

All of that training! She chastised herself as she bounded away from certain, terrible death. *And these things that should be dead are able to catch up to you, come on! Push!*

Her body burned and ached in protest to her exertions, her breath wheezed—her ribs were probably broken—but she carried on.

She had to keep looking back over her shoulder to get a sense of where her predators were, as she could not hear her tormentors in the vacuum. Every time she looked, her panic was renewed as the ravenous pack was that much closer. She clambered over the lip of the crater and gasped as her leg was caught. She turned to find a werewolf had reached over the lip and grabbed her ankle. With lightning fast reflexes, she jabbed down at it with her broken spear. The beast snarled silently, spewing boiling blood and spittle, and recoiled. It tumbled down the incline only to be replaced by the two dozen other werewolves.

She bolted for the rover that was only a couple hundred meters away. But she knew—even as the werewolves crested the rim of the crater and swarmed her—she never really had a chance.

Closing her eyes, she remembered her conversation with Isao not fifteen minutes ago. She decided to choose one painful death over another. Before the first werewolf reached her, she dropped her spear, disengaged her suit's safety features, and ripped her visor up.

The air was sucked out of her lungs so quickly she couldn't even gasp as they collapsed with a sickening crunch, heard only through her reverberating bones. Her skin blistered and boiled without heat, and her vision wavered white before she embraced the comfort of oblivion.

The werewolves tore her apart as they reached her anyway, not content to leave her body unviolated. As they ripped her suit apart and fed on the freeze dried remains of the poor, dead Griffin, the Alpha among them gazed across the greyscale surface. The intense moonlight pierced his retinas, seared his soul, and drove a vicious fury to feed, kill and to protect his territory with as much savagery as he could muster. His thoughts were clearer lately, ever since they injected that serum into him. So he knew he should be dead, as should his pack—such was the horrendous pain the void inflicted upon them—but the curse, the curse drove them beyond what was capable. It spoke to him with more power out here on the surface of his torment than it ever did in the base, or on Earth. So close to the fuel of his dark entrapment, it would not let them die to something as trivial as an inhospitable cosmos.

Only silver could break that hold; only silver could free the damned.

And even through the induced fury, even through the mind breaking pain of the vacuum, he caught sight of the lights in the distance, where the lunar colony Amenitude sat on the horizon.

Territory. The dreadful voice within whispered to his knowing mind. *Feed. Kill.*

He howled in silence, and despite the fact they could not hear him, his pack howled in tandem.

***

BHANU EVERLY

The doors hissed open and Diondre sped through them as Bhanu swept in behind him. They surveyed the habitat with quick, measured arcs, looking down the barrels of their silver spears.

Nothing.

The living quarters were the innards of the habitation dome that was attached to one side of Sigma Base. The apartments within were put together like temporary office blocks on a construction site. They were mass produced cubes of white, fitted together with all of the amenities one would need for an extended stay, and stacked on top of one another up to three stories high. The encapsulating, radiation safe dome had a transition glass finish for the times when the unfiltered sun was hitting the base directly. A dome was the most important feature of any good habitation space. It ensured a constant view of the landscape in order to help combat the cabin fever one would experience on such a base. Through the dome, the greyscale basin of the crater loomed up before them with shafts of harsh sunlight streaking down to ricochet off the glass, scattering into dazzling rainbow streaks that dwindled into the eternal night.

Among the cubicle habitats beneath the dome were well tended hydroponic gardens. There were all manner of tall stalks and bushels as well as vertical veggie racks—a taste of home and a much needed luxury for well to do establishments on the Moon.

"Well, this is nice," Bhanu commented. "Shame about the blood spatter." She tapped her foot on the ground, doing so without the humming click clack of metallic boots to draw her down. "Ah, no metallic flooring here, all pebble."

"Captain, transponder, two units down, third storey."

"Take point, New Guy."

"Ma'am," Diondre muttered.

He bounded down a path of square silicon pavers set into a floor of Moon gravel, sweeping the laneways made by the clustered units while Bhanu kept her eyes on the tiny balconies above for movement. Every so often she would glance at him, perplexed at his stiff movements in defiance of the lighter gravity.

"Diondre, you need to stay calm."

"I am calm," Diondre said through gritted teeth.

"You're practically hyperventilating. What happened?"

"Nothing, ma'am. Let's just get to the transponder."

Bhanu squinted at Diondre, but they were too exposed out here for her to press further. She continued on in his wake without comment.

After a moment of tense bounding, they reached the unit block in question. It had a smear of blood trailing up the zigzagging staircase that hugged the block. Diondre stepped onto the staircase and his boot clicked to the first step. The magnetised flooring was in place, so they marched with a painfully audible click-clack beat up the stairs in short order, reaching the door to the top apartment.

Bhanu banged on the door, shouting "Griffins, open up!"

There was no answer. Bhanu nodded to Diondre.

He took a step back and butted the door control mechanism with his spear gun. It fizzled and the door slid open—no need for impressive home protection on a secluded base.

They moved into a dark living space. It was a cluttered mess, with a pile of furniture forming a makeshift barricade between the door and the living room.

"Stay back!"

A woman with a Greek accent reached over and sprayed the Griffins with a canister that expelled silver particulates.

"Ma'am," Bhanu said, and waved through the silver cloud, unfazed, with her visor still drawn down. She then rammed through the furniture which fell with comical slowness. "Ma'am, we're the rescue squad."

The woman—a scientist in a ragged, bloodied lab coat with frizzy brown hair and olive skin—sprayed Bhanu in the face again. Diondre stepped in and batted the canister from her grasp; it fell to the ground, as well as a data pad she was gripping in her other hand.

"Doctor Helena Maragos?" he took her by the shoulders and steadied her, gazing into her eyes.

Bhanu cocked her head.

Helena calmed down and nodded. "Yes—God, sorry. I'm so glad you're here!"

"Hang on." Bhanu reached down and snatched up the data pad that Helena had dropped. She quickly looked over the screen and her eyes narrowed on the scientist, looking for a name tag, an ID badge, anything. "You've caused a lot of drama for my team, Doctor." She turned to Diondre. "And how the hell did you know her first name?"

Diondre turned to Bhanu, a shocked expression quickly turning quizzical. "What do you mean? Gaz said she sent the distress beacon, and her name came up on the transponder readout in the maintenance room."

"Gaz said Doctor Maragos, the transponder just gives a title and last name . . ." Warning bells were going off in Bhanu's mind; something wasn't right.

Helena looked between the two Griffins, a knowing expression on her face. "She's got you there, soldier."

"Ah," Diondre sagged. "Shit." He launched into Bhanu, ramming the tip of his silver spear into her chest as he drove her out the door and into the balcony railing while holding down the trigger. "This wasn't the plan, Captain."

"Griffin, what the fu—ARGH!" Bhanu went rigid with pain as Diondre's silver spear ripped through her, penetrating suit and flesh, piercing out through her back before it halted, embedded in place.

Her vision was a kaleidoscope of white and red spots, bright lights, and looming darkness. Her breath was a slow, pained wheeze and she sagged down only to be held suspended in a half crouch as the tip of the spear protruding from her back caught on the top of the railing. The pain was excruciating, but it paled in comparison to the hot fury that bubbled within her.

Diondre—her soldier, her betrayer—sighed and reloaded his silver spear as he turned back to the all-too-calm scientist.

"This your first time undercover, soldier?"

Bhanu's eyes twitched to follow them. Even as her consciousness faded, she had to know why this happened.

"No, but this is the first time I've walked into a shit show because people didn't do their job."

"What are you saying?" Helena crossed her arms.

"I was told the subjects would have been vented well before we got here. I was told you would already be in the rover and probably already at Amenitude with the data. But I arrive and find the place is actually overwhelmed—what the hell happened? This was not the plan!"

"I *did* vent them!" Helena snapped back. "They survived and tore their way back in! I had to let them in just to stop them from rupturing the base with constant breaches."

"You studied them for years. You didn't know they could survive in the vacuum?"

"Well, maybe I would have conducted an outrageous experiment like that if I had time. But there was a Pantheon agent with the research staff and he was catching on. I had to accelerate my schedule, and that meant acting blind to the werewolves' full capabilities. Thankfully I slaved the maintenance room controls to that data pad and managed to redirect them back to familiar territory in the cell blocks. I only got here safely by controlling their pathways, using the suppression systems, and crawling through vents. When you lot arrived, I wasn't sure if you were Sect or Pantheon, so I split you up."

Diondre found the data pad that Bhanu dropped when he attacked her. "Praise Him that the Sect got to you first. I'm the only agent we could embed on such short notice. As far as I know, the rest of the Griffins on site aren't Pantheon. I can't speak for anyone back at Amenitude. Though, it makes sense that the Pantheon would send *someone* else. Do you know what the rest of the Griffins are up to?" he asked as he typed away on the data pad, slaving it to his suit's wrist computer.

"The two in the cell blocks are dead . . . they vented *most* of the werewolves. The two in the lab are alive, and last I checked, heading for secure storage."

"Well, they're on their own. Come on. Let's get to the rover."

"That's not going to work, soldier. I've got copies of the data, but I haven't got the serum yet. Without it, the Sect's plan will be set back years. It's unacceptable to abandon it without at least trying to acquire it."

Diondre swore under his breath. "Fine, we try to get the serum. But if there are any complications, we bail with the data only. That's my call to make as the soldier, *scientist*."

Helena scoffed. "I agree, *if* the serum becomes too costly to acquire, it and all other considerations become secondary to this data." She handed Diondre a data stick. "That means you, that means me. This is a backup copy I made; better not to put all our eggs in one basket."

Diondre took the data stick and shoved it into his leg pouch.

A sadistic smirk crept across Helena's face.

"What?"

She pointed to Bhanu. "That Griffin is still alive."

Diondre turned and swore again, marching over to the twitching Bhanu. She keyed her comms with slow, clumsy movements. But all she heard in response was static. She could not even warn her team. Diondre stopped before her and tossed the data pad over the railing. Bhanu looked up at him, and her eyes shone with fury even as her face drained of colour. She still did not understand.

"Well, Captain . . . nothing personal." Diondre reached down and hefted Bhanu by her armpits even as she protested weakly. Then he tossed her over the railing.

Bhanu gasped a wet cry as the ground rushed up to meet her, and her world went dark.

KIERAN AHMAD

The muscle tensing fear was constant, the aching pain from the battle was constant, and the indomitable patter of Floof's tail wagging against his leg was constant. "What kind of twisted hell is this place?" Kieran lamented.

Floof barked happily in response.

"Aw, is little Kiery feeling sore?" Aideen mock pouted as she limped alongside him.

"If you ever call me Kiery again, I will eviscerate you. I'll also make sure every werewolf in the vicinity is dead so that I know you will bleed out rather than be mercifully fed upon."

"Bitch please, we both know I'd kick your arse." She took another step and stumbled, gripping at the wall.

"Are you sure they didn't bite you?"

"What kind of knob head do you take me for? I would tell you if I got bit, I just did in me leg, that's all. Tweaked it while trying not to be ravished upon by a group o'fuckers that looked marginally better than the last dickhead who tried to hit on me at the pub."

There was a vicious howl and they pivoted to aim down the white lit corridor.

"No responding howls; it's just the one," Kieran said.

"Bah, just one my arse!" Aideen tapped on her wrist pad.

"What are you doing?" Kieran glanced over her shoulder to her wrist pad. It showed a black and blue schematic of Sigma

Base with moving red dots in the laboratory and habitation dome.

"With the power on, I managed to tap into the local network—very limited access, we got motion sensors for lab and hab only. I'll be able to pick up maintenance control if we get a little closer. Cell blocks wouldn't connect. I hope Solvi and Isao are all right."

"They're Griffins," Kieran replied, "They'll be all right. What does the network say?"

"Movement in the lab indicates more than one o'the bastards—not many though. Maybe the others are dusted up still from your fisticuffs." She shot him an amused look. "Hab indicates two signals moving towards the secure vault, same as us. Must be Cap'n and the new guy."

"What's that third dot staying in habitation?" Kieran pointed at the motionless red blip on the blue and black map. It was quickly fading from view, as if it hadn't moved since it tripped the motion sensor.

"The scientist?" Aideen theorised. "Can't see why they'd leave them there though . . ." she was cut off by another howl from the lab—louder and closer than the first.

"Safe!" Floof wagged his tail and scurried down the hallway. "Safe is here!"

"I'm inclined to agree with the dog," Aideen said. "Werewolves are in the opposite direction."

"I think he meant the secure vault. Keep an eye on our backs." He grabbed Aideen around the shoulders and half hobbled, half hauled her down the corridor to a junction with a secure storage room set into the wall. It had secure metal mesh windows and appeared to be an armoury of sorts. A *buffer between habitation and the cell blocks, perhaps? Load of good it did them,* Kieran thought as he regarded the blood and viscera that lined the floors and walls in more concentration by the door.

Kieran keyed the access panel using a G.R. override and hoped it would work. The panel flickered green and the door slid open. Kieran dragged Aideen inside and keyed the door to close as Floof scurried in. As the door slid shut, the howls reached the hallway and a werewolf bounded down it, slamming into the mesh windows which rattled as it raked its claws across them. The werewolf recoiled as its claws burned.

"Heh, silver mesh, eh?" Kieran mused.

The interior was a small room, lined with gas cylinders on one end marked with red warning labels and a designation in bold, black lettering that read '*AgO2DET.*' The canisters were hooked up to pipes that laced through the ceiling. There were half empty weapon racks sporting the next to useless silver pellet guns, a large iron vault welded into the corner, and a small medical station.

There was a second hatch on the far side of the room that was marked as the path to the habitation dome. It slid open and the two Griffins rounded with their weapons up, but they held fire when Diondre walked in.

"Pleb!" Aideen shouted. "Never thought I'd be glad ta see ya, and . . . you're not Cap'n?"

A frazzled looking scientist shambled through the door and Floof raced up to her, barking as the voice collar yelled, "fren!" over and over.

"Oh, not this fucking dog again!" the scientist rubbed her brow as if massaging away a migraine. "One failed experiment to communicate with a werewolf in its transfigured state and I'm left haunted by a mongrel mascot."

Diondre gestured to the scientist who pushed past Floof. "This is Doctor Maragos," he said, and hesitated. "Helena." Diondre then gestured to Kieran and Aideen. "These are the squad mates I was telling you about."

"Pleasure," Kieran said. He gestured to the gathering werewolves snarling on the other side of the mesh. "Now would you mind telling me what IN THE FUCK WERE YOU THINKING?"

"And where is Bhanu?" Aideen asked, her eyes narrowing.

"The Captain is gathering data still in the maintenance control room," Diondre said.

Aideen glanced at her wrist pad.

"I'm here to get the serum," Helena said, stalking past the two Griffins. "If the three of you wouldn't mind keeping an eye on our friends, we can get this and be off." She started typing a code into the access panel on the large iron safe in the corner, the one next to the canisters of gas.

"What's all these—weapons?" Kieran asked, motioning to the canisters.

"Not quite, Griffin," she said as the safe beeped. "It's pressurised silver powder."

"You put metal particulates in an oxygen aerosol?" Aideen cried. "You lot *are* mad. If those things get scratched, you can expect this whole place to go kaboom."

"That's why they're voice activated and can only be dispersed in small increments."

"Look, lady, something ain't right about you." Aideen raised her silver spear to draw a bead on the scientist.

"While I don't approve of aiming weapons at civilians, she has a point." Kieran eyed Diondre, whose fingers were twitching along his own silver spear as beads of sweat formed on his brow, visible even under his visor.

"Care to explain yourselves, Griffins?" Diondre said, "Mission was search and rescue."

"Technically, our first priority was seek and destroy." Kieran replied.

"I tapped into the motion sensors," Aideen said, "There is no movement at maintenance control. Where the fuck is Bhanu?"

Diondre sighed. "She's prepping the base's rover, it's right by maintenance control."

One of the werewolves snarled, taking another rake at the silver mesh screen to no effect.

Kieran raised his silver spear and trained it on Diondre. "You said she was gathering data a moment ago."

The sweat was dripping from Diondre's face.

"Soldier," Helena said, and straightened. "These Griffins are too switched on for your rattled mind." She looked between the Griffins, Aideen had her weapon trained on her, and Kieran was still aiming at Diondre. "Remember what we said. While it might set them back, what Sect really needs is the research I already gave you. All other considerations are secondary."

"What the fuck is the Sect?" Aideen said.

"Ma'am, are you sure?" Diondre raised an eyebrow. He backed up to the door and Kieran gestured with his spear that it was a bad idea.

Helena looked between Kieran and Aideen before answering. "The data you have is all that matters. I can provide nothing that the data does not. You gave yourself access to the system, soldier. Use it," Helena said resolutely.

Diondre looked between them and nodded. "By your hands, He shall be set free," he said reverently as he slowly tapped his wrist pad.

"By my hands, the scales shall be set right," Helena responded.

"What in the ever-loving fuck are you two on about?" Aideen started to say.

But Diondre keyed the system to open the other door, the one behind Kieran. As it slid open—as the werewolves surged through and overwhelmed the Griffins from the rear—Diondre slipped out the way he came.

Part 7: Search and Rescue

BHANU EVERLY

The stars were dim, scattered across a foggy surface. Every stabbing breath clouded them further. A red light blinking beneath the helmet's rim indicated a systems failure—no internal air conditioning to keep the visor clear from the effects of humidity.

Bhanu coughed and groaned herself back into consciousness. More condensed breath fogged her view of the habitat dome as she looked through her visor, past the butt of the silver spear that protruded from her chest and up the three storey living block she was thrown from.

How come I'm not dead? Sure, the spear embedded in her chest cavity was probably keeping some vital fluids from leaking out too quickly—for now—but the fall should have killed her.

She pulled open her visor and breathed the relatively fresh air of the dome, shifting in the Moon pebbles to get her bearings. Bits of dust and gravel tumbled slowly in the wake of her sluggish movement.

"Ah," she grunted. *Lower gravity, softer fall. Still, doesn't help that I was skewered.*

The data pad Diondre tossed over the railing was nearby. *My team.* She reached for the device, fumbling with bulky hands. "Fuck this." She tore her glove off, suffering the cold as the suit no longer kept her skin compressed—temperature controls in the base were standard, she must have lost quite a bit of blood to experience such a chill. A lukewarm sensation was seeping through the inside of her suit. *Shit*. She gripped the data pad with clammy fingers, accessed the station's systems, and found life signals in secure storage not twenty paces away. There was a lot of movement on the screen. Then there was a vicious howl, followed by a shout.

Spear wound or not, she was a Griffin, a captain, and her team needed her. She gritted her teeth and pushed up to her feet with a yell, grabbing her spear gun and using it as a makeshift crutch. The pain was unbearable; her vision wavered, and she couldn't think straight. She fumbled for a device in her hip pouch, pulling out an injection module. She pressed it into her neck and gasped.

Adrenaline flooded through her system via the combat stimulant and the pain ebbed somewhat. Her vision cleared well enough, and she soldiered on.

Every step was another skewering wound through her body as her muscles and tendons flexed against the invasive object in her chest. Every breath—every heave to keep on going—caused her vision to throb with white lights and tinges of red in her periphery. She did not have long.

But she had already lost a Griffin on her last mission—*poor Jason*—and she assumed she already lost Isao and Solvi if that bitch Helena was to be believed. She was not going to abandon the rest of her team when a wolf had slipped into their midst, tarred and feathered to blend in, and obviously an imposter in hindsight. Her team was just too bereaved from recent losses to pick up on the signs.

"Oh God." *Was Roshni a plant too? Was Lucas back on the Hippogriff with a double agent sitting by his side, or would he already be dead?* "It doesn't matter," she told herself through a clenched jaw. *First, save who you can.*

There was a howling commotion. Down the alley between two living units, the pressurised door that led from the habitation dome into the research station slid open. Diondre tore through it, tripping and dropping his weapon clumsily, and was then up and running as he grabbed it by the shoulder strap.

"Traitor!" Bhanu yelled. She hefted her silver spear and squeezed the trigger.

Diondre looked up in shock, skidding to a stop from an awkward moon sprint. As he skidded, he kicked up pebbles and dust to obscure Bhanu's vision before dashing in another direction—through to the maintenance control room.

Bhanu tracked his shape through the dust cloud as her spear whistled free. There was a cry as the shaft struck a glancing blow on his leg, but he continued bounding around the dome to reach his escape.

Bhanu screamed as she reached around her body, pulling out another spear to fit into her gun, and bounded for the door Diondre had slipped out of. There was still a commotion within, screeches, howls and an enraged roar that could only have been Kieran.

She threw herself across the low gravity space and collapsed into the corridor as her magnetic boots simulated Earth-G.

With a cry she pushed herself up, and her eyes widened in horror at the scene unfolding before her.

Kieran was on his back with several of the werewolves tearing chunks out of his suit and armour, tearing chunks out of his flesh. He was keeping them at bay through pure will, and would soon succumb. Aideen was trapped beneath him, bowled over when the pack of beasts surged through the other door. Floof was in the corner barking, and the scientist was in another corner, screaming in agony as a werewolf with a wounded shoulder disemboweled her at its leisure.

Bhanu's eyes hardened as she focused on the canisters lining the far wall. They were marked with chemical signs she could not decipher, save for the symbols for silver and oxygen. In her failing state, she drew the only conclusion she cared for, and took the risk—the risk of dying in silver fire versus dying under tooth and claw.

She raised her silver spear and fired. The spear flung through the air with a heralding whistle and struck the top of a canister. It hissed and sparked as metal screeched through metal, and the pressurised oxygen ignited, exploding upwards and spreading across the ceiling in a burst of iridescent flame. It rolled across the top of the room like a wave, inverted, discoloured, wrong, and surreal.

The werewolves howled in fury. One looked up at the last moment and copped the blast directly in the face. The wave of flame seared its fur to ash as the coursing silver particulates sanded it down to the bone in an instant. The werewolf dropped dead as its writhing body shrivelled into that of a wretched old man.

Most of the surviving werewolves retreated as fire and silver precipitate assailed them. They tore out the door they came through and screeched all the way down the hallway to the lab. But the last one—the one with the wounded shoulder that was eviscerating Helena—snapped around to leer at Bhanu even as the flame consumed its shaggy mane, even as the silver burned through its flesh. It lunged for her with a snarl of malice. It dug its claws into her shoulders and raised her up into the flame that was pooling *up* in the ceiling.

Her reflexes—aided by combat stimulants—kicked into gear. Bhanu had just enough time to pull the slide of her visor down as the flames assailed her compromised suit. Heat and pain—that was all there was to experience—but it was not enough to break her while she knew her Griffins were still in danger.

She gripped the base of the spear protruding out of her chest and wrenched it free with a battle roar as the iridescent flames cascaded over her helmet. The butt of the weapon gouged out the snarling werewolf's eye and it recoiled with a high pitched yelp. It dropped Bhanu to the ground and she fell in a heap. The creature retreated over her into the habitation dome.

The world was going dark, even as the silver flakes fell around her like radiant snow. They danced lazily in the lunar-G, spurred into pirouettes and eddies by currents of heat from the roaring flames that still spilled from the canister. The fail safes had contained the combustion to the one storage unit, but that would not last for long.

"At least I tried," she whispered with a trembling lip, curling into a ball to die. *And at least that's pretty,* she thought, watching the sparkling, silver flakes fall.

"Captain!" Aideen was crawling out from under the incoherent Kieran, "Ev, Bhanu, are you alright?"

The light returned to her, focus forced its way into her mind, *I'm not done yet.* "Aideen," she groaned, "the valves."

Aideen pulled herself the rest of the way out from Kieran and stumbled under the ceiling of flame to the canisters. She found the offset valve and twisted it until the flame was replaced by a layer of thick smoke on the ceiling. The silver particulates still drifted down around them, which meant the werewolves would not enter—for the moment.

"Captain," Aideen said, turning from the valve.

"Kieran first," Bhanu commanded. She pulled herself into the room properly, her suit smoking from her encounter with the werewolf.

"Right, shit." Aideen crouched over Kieran, pushing Floof out of the way as he too tried to help. "He's been infected, Bhanu." Her voice was a barely suppressed sob. "He's cursed." She rallied her nerves and pulled out a dual purpose medi-foam canister from her chest pouch. She started sealing Kieran's wounds with the foamy beige substance. It filled into the gaps in his flesh and hardened into a protective bandage layer, it also formed a seal around his broken suit. "It's all right Kieran, it's over, hush now."

"I'm bitten," he coughed. "I'm cursed, damned. Save the foam."

"Why don't you shut the fuck up?" Aideen said as she continued smothering his open wounds with the foam, and coating any dinged or cracked part of his suit.

"Diondre is heading for the station's rover." Bhanu slumped against the wall next to the barely conscious Helena, whose innards were spilling out of large red gashes in her gut. "Who are you, and how did you plant someone in Global Response, let alone in the Griffins?"

Helena's pale, drained face perked up slightly in smirk. "We are the Cronos Sect," she coughed. "And your Griffins are play things to the real warriors in this fight."

Bhanu pulled out the data pad that had control of the base. "I'm going to trap that imposter in here with us."

Aideen finished plying Kieran with medical foam and rushed over to check on Bhanu. "What about Isao and Solvi?" Aideen said as she looked closer at Bhanu's open wound and grimaced. Blood seeped freely from it; the combat stimulant was wearing off, and now that Bhanu had torn the spear from her body, there was nothing plugging the wound.

"I already know the wound is fatal, Aideen. Our teammates are dead, isolated by this bitch to be picked off by the beasts she released."

Aideen took an instant to process that. Her face fell for a second and then her mind went to work on solving the situation, her eyes lighting up. Bhanu always appreciated that about Aideen; no matter how bad the situation got, she found a way through it.

"The serum." Aideen went to Helena's dying body and found the injection module. It was a small white rectangle with a red measured vial wedged within it and an injection cap on one end. She rushed over to Kieran and jammed it into his neck. He twitched and grunted in response.

"She said that doesn't stop it," Kieran mumbled.

"But you only just got bitten," Aideen said, "They only tested it on the turned so far. Maybe it will work differently."

"It doesn't matter," Helena coughed. "We'll all die here, and the Sect will create an army of wolf men to defeat the Pantheon once and for all."

"Ignore her, Griffin," Bhanu said as Aideen turned on Helena with clenched fists. "Diondre made it to the rover and is heading for the lunar base . . . but I can un-jam our comms." She tapped on the data pad, finally patching the Griffin's comms into Sigma's system. "Lucas, come in."

There was a burst of static and the familiar voice clicked over the radio, "Well, thank fuck for that. What the hell is going on down there?"

"Down there?" Bhanu said. *Thank God he's alive.* "Where's Roshni?"

"Roshni stayed behind at Amenitude to coordinate the evacuation. Ev, the terminal has been breached by a huge pack of werewolves. We don't know how, but they tore their way in from the outside. All the station's outer defences were ineffective—no silver munitions—and the calibre was meant to shred space suits, not tear through whatever roided up leather those beasties are made of. They got in without any losses. I took off in the Hippogriff in the confusion to come rescue you, figured shit hit the fan. I'm circling the research base now, a rover took off a minute ago, and the Amenitude rover you drove here is parked on the crater rim still, near a . . . well, it looks like a body."

"Okay, Lucas." Bhanu forced her dying mind to operate on sheer willpower. "Circle around to the habitation dome. You need to pick up Kieran and Aideen. We have suffered heavy casualties. Diondre betrayed us and you need to stop him, and maybe Roshni, from escaping."

"What about you?" Aideen said.

"Yeah, Ev, what Aideen said," Lucas echoed.

"I'm done for. I'm going to make sure this whole station goes up in silver flames, and the remaining werewolves with it."

"But, Ev!"

"But nothing, Lucas! Our priorities are the same. Search and rescue is soon to be done, Diondre has the data—now all that is left is to seek and destroy. So pick up our remaining Griffins at the habitation dome, eliminate the remaining werewolves in the terminal, and run that bastard down!"

"Ev . . ." Aideen said, biting back her arguments. "How are you going to blow up the base?"

Bhanu eyed the canisters. "The same way I nearly blew it up the first time. I'll give you and Kieran five minutes, and then I'm blowing this place to hell—properly."

"What about the scientist?"

"Fuck her. She did this. She will die with me if she doesn't bleed out beforehand."

Aideen looked hard at Bhanu. She hoped her captain wouldn't see her lip quivering through their visors, but she knew better. "It was an honour, Captain."

"Aideen, it was my great pleasure." Bhanu straightened even as she winced and tapped the readout on her wrist, starting a timer. "Five minutes. Get to Lucas, and get out of here."

AIDEEN KELLY

Aideen swore as Bhanu started the countdown. She went to Kieran, helping him to stand by throwing his arm over her shoulder.

"Floof, out that way." Aideen pointed through the corridor that Bhanu had come from.

"But the big toothy boy is out there. I can whiff him good, he's waiting." Floof inched up to the corridor but didn't venture further.

Kieran mumbled something incoherently. Aideen heard the words, "... mess him up for you," but she ignored it.

"You've saved me twice, Kieran, now it's my turn."

She held her silver spear underarm as she half dragged him through the corridor, pausing to take one last look at Bhanu, who waved her on with steely determination.

"Lucas," Aideen said as she moved through the corridor without another word to her captain. Floof followed tentatively. "Lucas, swing around the habitation dome. I've got Kieran with me and one survivor. The LZ will be hot."

"Roger that. I see one external air lock on the west side of the dome; I'll swing around there. Hurry up, lassie."

"Can you dock with the airlock?"

"Unknown. There should be EVA suits by the dock for your survivor if you can get there in time."

Aideen glanced down at Floof. "We'll think of something." *Might need to bag him in a suit.*

The corridor was clogged with thick, sparkling smoke thanks to Bhanu's rescue. Aideen's sporadic breathing came in quick rasps as she strained to aim her silver spear at the changing shapes in the haze, made all the harder while she tried to manoeuvre herself and the wounded Kieran while balancing on her good leg.

They reached the end of the corridor and found themselves in the habitation dome. Their boots unlocked from the ground, which made hauling Kieran easier. Aideen turned for the west side of the dome, moving through the multi-storeyed units. She half shuffled, half bounded between the alleys as the smoke cleared through the filtration systems, twitching the tip of her spear in each direction as her mind taunted her with darting shapes and shadows. She kept squeezing the trigger, letting the gasses build up, but then easing off before the firing sequence triggered, hoping that if the werewolf did leap out at her she could fire off a quick shot without the wait time.

This isn't right, Aiden lamented, moving through the units. Griffins were trained to battle the horrors of the unknown on a regular basis, monsters of legend, spirits, cults, and the odd inter-dimensional being. But this was different; subterfuge, double agents? That was stuff for spooks and spies. It was all too much. And now she found herself alone. Aideen always had her fellow Griffins to back her up, but now it was just her.

Poor Jason. She thought on how scared he must have been in the end, on his own in that stupid ruin, surrounded by an unknown *human* enemy. *Poor Solvi, Isao, and Bhanu.* Kieran mumbled incoherently and she bit down on her ruminating thoughts. She still had a teammate to get out of here, she still had a cursed beast to fight. That was something she could handle.

The Hippogriff swooped silently into view above, swinging around to face her from the west side of the dome. And *I still have a Griffin to back me up.*

It was a bulky ship, resembling an oblong box with curved edges. There was a protruding cockpit from the main fuselage that looked like a curved beak with twin-linked, underslung machine guns on a pivot point beneath it. It had four manoeuvrable thrusters, one on each corner, two armed, elegant retractable wings that resembled their namesake's, and a long aerodynamic tail with its own flaps and thrusters which would be useful in the Earth's atmosphere.

"Aideen—I see ya, lassie, I see ya. Keep moving."

"Do you see the werewolf?"

"Negative, I cannae use thermal readings either. They can't make it through the vacuum between the dome and the Hippogriff."

"This whole operation was doomed from the start."

"Don't think like that; we've got to get you out of there. Where's the survivor?"

"It's the dog, you nitwit."

Floof barked at her heels.

"God damn it, Aideen. I know you're in a stressful situation, but a bit more cohesive communication would be . . . ohhh fuck, big hairy bastard scaling the building on your right. He's on the roof!"

"Crap." Aideen pivoted and trained her spear on the rim of the structure on her right while still shuffling towards the airlock. "Talk to me, Lucas."

"He's prowling just out of your line of sight. I think he knows you're going for the exit, and you'll have to break cover to get there."

"Fuck, fuck, fuck," Aideen swore as she reached the edge of the block of structures.

Beyond an empty space was the curved outer edge of the dome with a square, metal airlock slotted into the clear surface. There was a row of space suits in lockers next to it, none that would fit a dog without coercion.

Aideen did some mental preparation. It would take about twenty seconds to haul Kieran over there, seconds to grab a spare suit for Floof, key the lock to open, get inside, and then close it again. The werewolf would definitely get them before then. She had to make her shot count.

"Aideen, you don't have much time."

"I know." Aideen took a big breath. "For the Griffins we've lost." She grabbed Kieran by the shoulders and bellowed as she tossed him across the distance.

In the Moon's low-G he glided gracefully for most of the short span before sliding across the rubble flooring, kicking up dust and pebbles as he ground to a halt. Aideen charged out after him the moment she threw him, catching up to him in a single bound and holding her silver spear close for the moment that was coming.

The werewolf snarled and leaped from the building, diving in slow motion through lunar-G for Aideen's position. Aiden dived over Kieran, squeezed the trigger as she turned mid flight and faced the terrifying visage of the hulking, hairy, clawed figure hurtling towards her.

Aideen steadied her resolve as the gasses built up in the firing chamber. The werewolf's claws were inches from digging into her. The spear flung loose, passing between its claws, through the hairs of its shaggy under mane with hissing smoothness and embedded in its rear quad.

It yelped and spun away, tumbling into the rubble. Aideen reached for another spear and swore when she found her quiver was not there—it had torn loose during the brawl in secure storage. The werewolf was howling as its leg sizzled, but it was not down. It was thrashing, rearing, and it sighted its prey with a vengeful yellow eye.

"Lucas, you need to open fire!"

"But Kieran's suit—is it sealed?"

"Swing by your firing vector and open the cargo hold." Aideen scooped Kieran into her arms, "Floof!" the dog barked and jumped over her shoulders and nuzzled between them. She squeezed them both close.

"You're crazy!"

The werewolf shook the Moon dust from its fur and prowled closer, its maw salivating as it growled—it knew its prey was now defenceless.

"JUST DO IT!"

Aideen backed up against the glass dome, the werewolf primed to leap, and she scrunched her eyes shut.

The dome's surface rippled with the sound of hail, she unclenched her eyes—the Hippogriff had swooped in above them and was firing upon the werewolf's position. The sustained strike chipped away at the dome's thick surface with high calibre weapons. Shell casings ricocheted away from the firing cannons in the vacuum as the dome shuddered, cracked, and finally, shattered.

Heavy silver rounds poured through the breach with the sound of a raging hurricane as the vacuum greedily sucked the atmosphere from the dome. The werewolf was pelted with fire, knocked back and shredded to pieces even as the units, the Moon dust and the hydroponic greenery was drawn up to the exploding dome ceiling within an instant, destroying it completely, and sucking Aideen, Kieran and Floof outwards at the same time.

Lucas had to make calculations on the fly. If he made one slight mistake, one unintentional twitch of the joystick, then Kieran and Floof would have jettisoned out into the lunar surface to die horribly as Aideen watched. But Lucas had lined up the shot with eerie perfection. The two Griffins, and Floof, were swept up in the tornado winds among debris and shrapnel. They slammed into the open cargo hold of the Hippogriff as it bucked and swayed in the torrent.

The doors to the cargo hold slammed shut as Lucas pulled away and he flooded the compartment with atmosphere. The hissing air filtered through the vents as the recently vented room pressurised and Aideen ripped her visor off to check on Kieran.

The place was a mess, armaments and gear were dislodged and scattered everywhere alongside debris and shards of glass from the dome.

Aideen found Kieran in the devastation and ripped off his visor too. His suit was mangled from the werewolves, but the foam would have sealed most of him in. His dark face was now pale and his head listed as lifeless eyes looked back at her.

"Kieran!" she cried as shook him. "Kieran, don't do this to me!" she slumped against his chest, sobbing, "Kieran, you're my best friend, please."

The burly chest had a spasm. Kieran coughed and wrapped his arms around the weeping Griffin. "Can I quote you on that?" his voice was weak, but his strong spirit shined through.

"Fuck you!" Aideen pulled back and whacked him. "Don't you ever get mauled by a pack of werewolves again!"

He laughed and coughed, wincing in pain. "That is something I've tried to avoid since I was just a boy. Did Floof make it?"

A pained bark sounded from under the wreckage. Aideen followed the sound and pulled an overturned table off the shivering dog. "Floof, are you okay?"

"I am in much hurt," the voice collar crackled, "but shall live if gib treats."

"Oh, baby, sweet baby." Aideen hugged Floof close. "I'm going to give you all the treats once this mess is over."

Floof barked weakly, but his tail started wagging.

"Hey," Lucas said over the intercom, "Are you all alive down there or what?"

Kieran groaned as he reached for his wrist pad to key the comms. "Aideen and I made it, Lucas—damned good flying."

"Yeah, for a Scotsman," Aideen said. "We owe you one. Pull back from the base. Bhanu will be blowing it shortly."

"Aye, a crying shame." Lucas said. "She was one of the best captains I ever did have."

"Bhanu," Kieran coughed. "If you're listening, we're free of the base. We'll stay here with you, until the end."

"You seem in better shape than a few minutes ago, sergeant," Bhanu said over the radio. "Better shape than me, anyhow."

"I think the werewolf venom is taking hold." Kieran said. "If I can hold it off long enough to hunt Diondre, then I will die a happy man."

"Good man." Bhanu started coughing. "Some of the other werewolves tried to come and get me. I fought them off easily enough with all the silver flakes around. I'll blow the silver canisters presently. Griffins, good hunting. For Isao, Solvi, Jason and Monica."

Part 8: Seek and Destroy

KIERAN AHMAD

The Hippogriff hovered in a holding pattern around Sigma Base. It seemed a quiet place on the outside, save for the ruined habitation dome, jettisoned cell blocks, and the wisps of silver smoke that hissed out of the failing seals.

Kieran and Aideen watched from a display screen in the cargo hold. Floof stood diligently by their side while Lucas watched from the cockpit. There was a spark from the section attached to the habitation dome, near where Bhanu was enacting her final testament. It was a quick flash of red and white that spurted out from the pressurised doors. The whole station rippled as it bulged outwards from the ignition point. The blast fissured out of the breaking seals and through windows all the way to the cell blocks before the base exploded with a violent, silent flash.

Aideen made the sign of the cross for her captain, her teammates, and the innocent staff that they could not save.

"Godspeed, Ev," Lucas said over the comms.

"Did any of the remaining werewolves on base make it out?" Kieran asked before doubling over with a pained snarl.

"Kieran?" Aideen rushed to his side and he pushed her off.

"Negative on that," Lucas said, oblivious to the altercation. "I'm scanning the blast zone with every conceivable technological and paranormal sensor we have onboard."

"Then all that remains is the colony. Get us to Amenitude, Lucas."

The Hippogriff pulled away from Sigma crater and jetted for the lunar colony.

"ETA five minutes; get your shit sorted Griffins. Opening a line with Roshni, she is hulled up with Gaz and a few survivors in the terminal. I'm getting some interference. This should take a moment."

"Keep the windows shuttered Lucas, it's the moonlight . . . I can't . . ." Kieran began. The windows in the cargo hold groaned shut. "Thank you."

Aideen and Kieran stripped off their bulky moon suits and discarded the clumsy silver spears—Aideen needed to help Kieran peel off the parts of his suit that had adhered to his wounds with medi-foam. The sticky tearing was like slowly ripping off a bandaid and made Kieran grit his teeth, but the wounds themselves looked as if they were months old, save for the dried blood.

"Kieran . . ."

"It's okay," he loaded a silver munitions mag into a handgun and racked the slide. He handed it to her. "Keep this one within easy reach. When the job is done, use it."

"Kieran, I . . ."

"You saw what those monsters were like, Aideen. But you haven't seen what they can do to the people they once cared about. The one that attacked my family, I knew him, beforehand. He was a good man, but he slaughtered his own daughters before turning onto the town; onto my brother." Kieran looked away. "I can't do that to you."

"But the serum?"

"You heard that recording the same as me. The serum just nullified some of their rage and reduced the time they spent transformed. The best case scenario is I survive and get captured by whatever fucking secret men's group Diondre works for. That's the *best* case. Worst case is I hurt someone who doesn't warrant it. Promise me you'll do me if it comes to it. Promise on this." He pulled out his digital gyroscope.

Aideen looked between the gyroscope and Kieran. "You can't ask me to do that."

"I'm not asking, I'm begging, on my faith."

Aideen placed her palm on the device that twisted and whirred internally as it kept track of Earth. "I swear, Kieran."

The two stood there a moment, the hum of the engines thrummed in the silence, then a sly smirk crept across Aideen's face.

"What?"

"You don't think I'd get excommunicated for swearing a sacred death vow on a Muslim gizmo do you? Murder and blasphemy, that's like, two strikes."

Kieran pushed her off with a laugh. "Cheeky."

They prepared for a combat insertion. First Aideen bandaged her leg and injected medi-foam of her own to help with pain and function. As they were gearing up, the display screen in the hold flickered to life.

An olive skinned woman in black and bronze Griffin fatigues with a golden insignia on the shoulder looked back at them with wide eyed concern. "Kieran, Aideen, Lucas filled me in. I'm so sorry for the team."

"Shut your mouth, Roshni, unless you're gonna answer this here one question," Aideen all but yelled. "Are you one of these—what was the name she used—Cronos Sect bastards?"

Roshni flinched. "I don't know what you're talking about."

"Don't fuck with me!" Kieran bared his teeth, which seemed larger and more pointed than usual. "You were assigned to our team the same as Diondre after we lost Jason, after Monica was injured. Was it your people who took them out so you could be slotted into our midst?"

"Sergeant, please, there is much you don't understand."

"Then make us understand."

"I can promise you I am not with the Sect. I am with those that oppose them."

"Well, first off, great work so far!" Aideen cut in. "And second off, I'm not fucking buying it!"

"Hey!" A second face appeared on the screen—Gaz, the U.G. Liaison on Amenitude. "Can you guys sort your issues after you get us out of here? An army of those monsters broke through one of the secondary hangars and breached the terminal. We managed to seal the terminal from getting spaced, but we also sealed all of those bastards in with us. The terminal is quarantined. We have several dozen known casualties and three holdouts other than the control tower where we are. We also don't have any silver armaments."

"We do," Kieran said, "lunar bureaucracy be damned. We'll be there in two minutes. Give us access to the airlock controls."

"You have a plan, Kieran?" Aideen said as she donned her Griffin space helmet.

"We're going to airlock cycle breach."

"Ballsy," Aideen whistled. "I'm all for it."

"What's a cycle breach?" Gaz asked.

"It's a dynamic entry from vacuum into a pressurised area when one has control of the . . ." Roshni started saying.

"It's a rough entrance for all involved!" Lucas cut her off. "So Gaz, I'd get word out to everyone in the terminal to hold on tight. All right, Griffins, we're swinging in by the secondary hangar. Once you're inside I'll do sweeps of the terminal, but I cannae guarantee air support like at the dome."

"That's all right," Kieran slid silver shells into a pump action shotgun. Even through gloves, he felt heat in his fingertips as he handled the precious metal. It was bearable enough. "Just do your sweeps and provide covering fire if you can when we need it. The terminal window panels should be fitted with emergency sealant shutters, but we should only rely on them as a last resort. Do we have a location on Diondre?"

"We confirmed him entering the terminal," Roshni said. "But other than heading for the main hangar to find a ship, I don't know where he will be."

"Sure," Aideen said. "At least he will be slower with his weapon and in that blasted moon suit. That gives us the advantage, against him and the werewolves."

"Hmm," Kieran reached for his helmet.

Their Griffin vacuum suits were much more practical than the bulky suits the Lunar Government had provided them with. They were sleek, black, and lined with microscopic reinforced armour plates that blended into the weave on either side. It was effectively vacuum sealed chainmail, with further bronze coloured plating layered over their legs, chest, shoulders, and forearms. The plating was sleek enough that they could fit over their tactical riggings like proper operatives. The helmets were snug—not unseemly moon suit domes—and fit closely to their heads. With the visors locked down in place, they formed hooked nose snouts in the shape of a beak—like a Griffin's. The visor lenses were bronze and flashed as their tactical overlays powered on. As with all of their gear, the golden Griffin insignia was displayed proudly on their left shoulder. There was no mistaking who they were, nor their purpose.

"You all right?" Aideen asked as they formed up on the rampart door. "Floof, get through the door." Floof barked and bounded for the door that led to the elevator and the rest of the Hippogriff. Aideen hit a button on the wall to seal the door after Floof's exit. "Well trained, that dog." Aideen nudged Kieran, "But not you, you all right?"

"My vision is lacking in colour," Kieran said. "And I could smell the whole team on this ship before I put my helmet on. I could smell Bhanu, Isao, and Solvi as if I was nuzzling into their necks. I could even smell Monica, and Jason." He sighed, but it came out as a long drawn growl. "And I scented Diondre." He gripped his weapons so tight he quivered. "Once we are inside, I'll take my helmet off. I should be able to find him."

"Excellent, you take point then," Aideen chuckled. "What about the moonlight?"

"I can resist it for a while longer. I'll have to."

"Griffins," Lucas said. The whole ship lurched as he swung the Hippogriff around for the cargo door to face the secondary hangar. The cargo bay hissed. "Pressure equalised. I'm popping the hatch. I've synced the Hippogriff's suit interface with

Amenitude's, so your boots should mag-lock automatically when you get inside."

The door lurched open and the two Griffins found the red ceramic door of the lunar base hangar before them. It was ripped to shreds, with debris and overturned ships and rovers within. Kieran snarled as the moonlight hit them, but he upped his lens opacity to its fullest. He and Aideen sped down the cargo ramp and across the lunar surface as fast as the lower-G would allow them. As the Hippogriff took off they dove in through the broken door.

"You're all right, Kieran, you're all right," Aideen said over the comms as their boots mag-locked to the floor and they sprinted towards the airlock on the far side of the hanger.

Kieran roared in response and keyed his comms to Roshni. "Roshni, cycling airlock in twenty seconds, brace!"

Roshni clicked the comms twice in acknowledgment.

Their weapons swept the area as they went, looking for werewolves that were left behind in the spaced room before the terminal was sealed. They found none, and no bodies either; the station personnel must have evacuated once the werewolves got past their defences.

Their boots clicked and clacked against the gunmetal surface of the hangar floor. The magnetic hum reverberated through their legs as their breathing quickened. The airlock doors ahead rushed closer as they advanced.

But Kieran heard more than their boots, and more than their breath in their helmets. His heart was in his ears—not beating, but bashing against his brain like a mallet upon a drum. His exposure to the Moon's surface had awakened something in him. And by Allah, he was going to use it to dismember anything that got in his path.

"Cycling!" he roared as they reached the first airlock.

It hissed open as he keyed the program with his HUD. The air within the compartment, not given time to equalise, rushed out to buffet them. But they were ready, and charged through the room's escaping atmosphere to keep sprinting through the pressurisation chamber. Once their suits recognised they had crossed the threshold, the door behind sealed and the one in front opened immediately.

The effect was instantaneous.

When the Griffins entered the tiny pressurisation chamber, they released a small amount of atmosphere into the void. But now they entered the terminal, the whole gargantuan compartment's air rushed for the vacuum of the smaller chamber. The entire space shifted like a blast wave swept through it, a pull towards the breach that no one was prepared for—no one but the Griffins charging through the pocket hurricane they had conjured. Stands were knocked over, eviscerated bodies were rolled once or twice, items and food and luggage tumbled end over end, and the werewolves—besieging the holdouts of people around the terminal—stumbled.

One by the door face planted with a surprised snarl. Kieran reached it before Aideen did. He ripped off his helmet, allowing his now shaggy beard to flow in the dying air currents. He leered down at his enemy as he shoved his shotgun into its face and pulled the trigger. The silver shot blew its head into oblivion.

Kieran screamed a guttural, primal, battle cry, cocking his shotgun. "The Griffins have swooped in to feed!"

The pack was spread throughout the terminal—a large open space that the Griffins had passed through when they first arrived at Amenitude. It had tiered levels ascending to the inner wall of the colony proper, each overlooking one another and providing a staggered, ascending view through the curved glass window that was the outer wall.

As before, the levels were filled with fast food restaurants, souvenir shops and '*outdoor*' eating areas on each balcony looking out over the grey lunar surface. Except now, amber warning lights flashed, red floor lights marked paths to safe havens and evacuation zones, and blood and litter was scattered across the tiles. The sun shone across on the Moon's surface and reflected as eerie pale silver into the chaotic terminal—the only proper illumination in contrast to the emergency lighting in the otherwise dim terminal. The silvery rays drove the werewolves into a perpetual frenzy, and drove Kieran further into depraved madness.

He scrunched his eyes shut—the transformation within him was not yet complete, but it was getting closer. *Not yet.*

Aideen swept up alongside him and opened fire with her snub-nosed submachine gun. She fired silver rounds in short bursts, downing a werewolf that was clambering up one of the tiered levels to slash at a screaming civilian who made a poorly calculated risk.

As it sounded its death knell, a returning call was echoed, a monstrous howl that rallied the pack throughout the terminal to focus on the new threat. Kieran understood the call, and was glad that they finally saw the Griffins as a foe to be reckoned with.

The two Griffins swept down the lower level, training their weapons upwards as the pack swarmed to face them. Aideen fired at one on the third level that dodged out of the way. She tracked it with her fire before her weapon clicked dry.

"Reloading!" she barked.

Kieran blasted one that was bold enough to leap down from the second level and pumped the slide on his shotgun. "Covering."

He fired several times at the upper levels as they shuffled down the terminal and Aideen quickly reloaded. Kieran relished the evened odds, but mused at how it was less satisfying when the spent shells fell slowly to the ground in lunar-G. Aideen tapped his shoulder and fired some quick bursts as Kieran slotted more shells into his weapon.

"They're pulling out of my line of fire," Aideen said. There was a scream above and a screech of struck metal. "And they're going back to attacking civilians."

"They're trying to make us come to them, within clawing distance," Kieran muttered, nodding to an escalator. "Let's not disappoint them."

They sped up the escalator to the second level. As they reached the top several werewolves leapt out at them. The first one was thrown back in the low-G by a blast from Kieran and the second slumped forward mid stride as Aideen put three rounds in its chest. It slid awkwardly before friction halted it. Every death resulted in their bodies shrivelling back to a human corpse.

The third werewolf made it through their fire and clawed at Kieran, knocking the shotgun from his hands. Kieran returned its snarl and drew a silver combat knife. He lunged in—taking a savage gash to the head without fear or flinching—and drove his knife up into the werewolf's neck. It burned through the flesh and seared the blood which burst out in coagulated clumps. Kieran threw the dying werewolf over his shoulder with a savage grapple manoeuvre, and the body tumbled down the escalator. He spun as Aideen fired at the werewolves on the third level and he threw his knife at them in a rage.

"Keep pushing up?" Aideen asked.

"I can smell Diondre's blood," Kieran said, pointing down the terminal and up several levels. "Let's follow his trail. If we make it look like we're running away, they'll give chase and leave the civilians in cover."

"Roger."

Aideen screamed and fired several wild bursts over the terminal while legging it down the terminal. Kieran pulled his assault rifle off his back and clicked it to full auto. The Griffins laid down covering fire in a leap frog formation, firing wild shots that went well over the werewolves' heads. Emboldened, the creatures pursued their apparently panicked prey.

The Griffins had bolted halfway down the terminal when a pack of werewolves leaped down and up at them from different levels ahead.

"Ambush!" Aideen shouted. She drew a smoke grenade from her rigging and threw it down ahead of her. A smoke screen burst into view, sparkling with silver flecks, and the ambushing werewolves retreated with snarls. Aideen and Kieran fired into the smokescreen blindly before turning and warding off their pursuers with precise shots that downed two more.

"We should be more careful next time," Aideen said as she slammed another magazine into her weapon. "Do you have a twenty on Diondre?"

"He's moved down a few levels and has gained distance on us. We need to get him before he can get to the main hangar."

"Right-o then—through the smoke." Aideen threw another silver smoke grenade over the current cloud, nodded with satisfaction at the enraged shrieks of the werewolves hiding on the other side, and charged into the smoke with a battle cry.

Kieran followed suit, but when he hit the silver smoke, his skin turned to fire. With a cry of surprised anguish he stumbled back, clutching at his scalding skin and wheezing as his lungs burned from the inhaled silver specks.

"Aideen!" he called after her with a rasp, but the sound of gunfire was his only answer. Did she know he could not follow her? He reached for his helmet before realising he had discarded it at the airlock. "Fuck, Aideen!"

The werewolves pursuing them sprinted past the smoke on the upper levels. She would soon be overwhelmed.

With a growl, Kieran leaped over the balcony railing, back to the first floor. His fall was stalled by the low-G, then accelerated as his mag-boots came closer to the tiling, making for a disorienting impact. But he had no time to be confused. He up and bolted down the terminal, following the sounds of gunfire while holding his hand up to his ear piece. "Aideen, respond, damn it!"

"A bit busy here, Kieran—where the fuck are ye?"

"Lower level—I couldn't get through the silver smoke. Where are you?"

"Well, shit, I just threw down a fuck-tonne more of the stuff. Formed a nice little defensive barrier, they can only get at me by trying to jump over it and into the clearing in the middle." There was another burst of fire and a dead werewolf slammed somewhat gracefully into the bottom floor ahead of Kieran. "Hah, you fucker, try again!"

"Visibility is poor through the smoke from up here, lads," Lucas said on the comms as the Hippogriff streaked by the curved glass exterior of the terminal. "But Aideen is definitely in a spot of bother."

Kieran snarled and sprinted past the shrivelling, dead werewolf and the silver smoke on the second level towards the next set of escalators. Aideen was surrounded, and the smoke would soon dissipate; he had to get to her.

He was halfway up the escalators when he stopped cold. Two levels up—aiming his silver spear down at him—was Diondre. Even within his bulky suit he nodded greetings before firing the spear at Kieran. Faster than he knew he could move, Kieran dodged to the side. The spear sailed past him towards the curved terminal window. It cracked on impact as the spear embedded in the thick screen.

"Kieran, I'm running out of smoke—where the hell are you?" Aideen screamed over the comms.

The cracks in the window wall spread, a hiss of atmosphere streamed into the void, then the cracks grew larger, and even more atmosphere vented, causing more cracks. Kieran's eyes widened as he realised the snowballing effect the failing integrity was generating. Then the whole pane shattered and he was pulled out onto the lunar surface in a torrent of air—without a helmet—and slammed into the Moon dust. He tore at his throat as the air was sucked from his lungs until they snapped and crumpled, as his eyes dried and shrivelled and bulged out of his head at the same time, as the sweat steamed from his blistering, shrinking skin.

He screamed without sound in the sudden silence. His earpiece buzzed as someone tried to talk to him—Aideen, surrounded by werewolves. The light reflecting off the Moon pierced his blurring vision, like a lance straight into his brain stem. Something snapped, his thoughts turned to dull rage and a voice—a feeling—spoke as an instinct in his dying mind. The curse was finally taking hold.

Feed—his body cracked as bones shifted and reformed—*Kill*—his organs ruptured as they stretched, twisted and grew to accommodate the new body that was emerging—*Territory*.

Three basic impulses throbbed through his awareness, and they could all be achieved by devouring anything that moved. All other thoughts waned as his skin—desiccating in the vacuum—stretched taut and sprouted fur, as his nose grew black before his face and his armour broke to accommodate his bulk.

An item tumbled from his crumbling armour, and its dancing, digital readout caught his suffering mind's eye—the gyroscope. It was pointing towards the horizon of the grey, dead world and the pained eye strained to follow the line to the Earth, which hung just within sight in the deep, black night.

His world, his faith, raged against the primal perversion cursing his soul. *Horrible things are just that*—his human mind told him—*things*. They could be resisted, just as he had resisted them, they could be overcome, just as he had overcome them, if only he held on to what he believed. Even though he was now turning into the beast that attacked his city, that killed his brother, he was still a man, still a follower of the word of Allah.

The blue dot winked at him, a beacon of focus and salvation, and even amongst the pain of death, space, and transformation, he began to formulate—not thoughts—but understanding.

As man turned to beast, as his lungs surrendered to the vacuum, as the universe stripped him of his bodily fluids through every pore and orifice, the recording left by Doctor Maragos came to his understanding. She said that a werewolf showed more mental capacity with the serum. But more than that, something else that was primal was discovered even before the serum was administered, something that the scientists did not have the imagination to tap, not yet. When placed together, the werewolves formed a pack bond. They would die to protect one another.

With the serum affecting his thoughts as a cursed beast, Kieran could force one conclusion into his fading mind. Aideen was a part of his pack, and those monsters were about to tear her limb from limb.

He bared his new fangs, turning back to the gaping hole in the lunar colony as the air rushed from it, as the blast shields slammed closed, and he charged for the narrowing gap.

He bounded effortlessly on limbs now longer, denser, and formed with unbreakable bone. They were strung together by tendons of iron and propelled by thick muscle fibres that bulged against one another, threatening to break through taut, leathery skin and shaggy grey and black fur. Kieran made it through the broken window in seconds, against the escaping torrents, and landed within the terminal as the emergency shield slammed shut.

He stood tall, and his hind claws—having broken through his boots—dug into the tile flooring to grant him purchase. His armoured trousers threatened to burst at the seams as they clung to him in tatters. His torn top and sturdy tactical rigging hugged his body, and he still had his assault rifle slung across his shoulder by the strap.

He whiffed—his lungs popping as his body forced them to expand back into place under unholy compulsion—sniffing at the air. The scents he could now smell were an explosion of sensation to counter the dulled colours of his vision, which brightened even the dim terminal to stark daylight. It was as if the moonlight ricocheted endlessly within the yellow, cursed venom swirling around in his irises.

The air smelled of fire, from hints of silver from the fighting. Kieran snarled as he realised his tattered tactical vest was still armed with the weaponised metal, but he had no time to discard it as other scents demanded his attention. Panic and fear permeated the space, blood and food, danger and threat, and the familiar bodily scent of a friend who was fighting for her life—Aideen.

Kieran snarled and leaped up the first level to where Aideen and a pack of werewolves were righting themselves after the sudden venting of atmosphere. The venting also siphoned away the silver smoke, and Aideen was desperately fumbling for her weapon on the ground. A beast was reaching for her with black clawed hands, and Kieran's defiant howl stopped it in its tracks.

The pack rounded on the challenger, on the outsider that was here to claim their prey for his own, and snarled in response. Deep down within the primal place that the human mind of Kieran was struggling to survive, he was drawn back to that dark street in Wellington—to the hulking, furry beast that slaughtered his brother, howling at the Moon. All Kieran had possessed was a silver dinner knife in feeble, trembling hands.

He only survived that night through tenacity and luck, and ever since had trained to not have to rely on luck, to not be feeble, to be able to match the terrors of the paranormal world with strength and calm, tactical instinct. Now his training, strength and knowledge were wielded through the lens of the very beast that motivated his training. And by Allah and all that was good in this universe, the beast that was within, that was now without, was going to show this pathetic pack just how terrifying a werewolf could truly be.

Kieran howled and charged forward, straight into the werewolves. Claws raked against tile as he galloped and launched himself through the air. He engaged the closest werewolf by digging his claws into its neck and wrenching without hesitation or remorse, severing the arteries and cracking the spine. Those who fight the paranormal world say that only silver can free the damned from their plight, but that's because they never had the ability to turn the damned upon themselves, until now. Kieran's claws did their job.

Kieran rolled over the now deceased werewolf and came up to counter a savage swipe with an elbow block. The strike stalled and the werewolf blinked in shock at the deft defence.

Clenching his paw, Kieran followed up with a return hook punch to the gaping werewolf's snout and mauled its exposed neck as his foe whiplashed to the side.

With his back exposed, a werewolf stepped forward and raked at his shoulder blades. Kieran struck backwards with a hook kick, bludgeoning and raking the abdomen of his attacker at the same time. Kieran then spun, drawing with a clumsy paw a silver smoke grenade from his tactical rigging. He slammed the smoke grenade into his winded foe's jaw and struck with an uppercut. As claw slammed into jaw, Kieran immediately shut his eyes and turned away in a crouch. The silver smoke exploded in the werewolf's jaws, burning its tongue, gums and teeth so horrendously that they fell out as charred husks of bone.

His enemy was shrivelling before he hit the ground. While crouched, Kieran swiped at the next werewolf's knee, dislocating it. The werewolf collapsed with a howl of pain. Kieran leaped up, savaging the werewolf in the face with a knee strike, and drew his second silver combat knife to slam it down into the beast's head.

The next to oppose him launched forward with bared fangs to clamp around his neck. Kieran reacted by punching forward into the werewolf's mouth and shoving his claws down its throat. With a whine, it tried to pull back from its attack, which was its downfall. It gave Kieran the time he needed to grip at the beast's inner throat and wrench, pulling out its Adam's apple.

Kieran crushed the fleshy trophy in his claws while snarling at the bewildered werewolf. Their yellow eyes drained of their moonlit ferocity as the body withered.

There was a terrible roar of anguish, and Kieran snapped his attention up to lock eyes with a werewolf perched on the upper levels. The Alpha of the pack leered down at him. It was larger and stronger, and snarled with more ferocity than any of the werewolves Kieran had fought up to this point, as a man or as a beast.

The cursed primal part of his mind screamed to acquiesce, to roll over and show his belly to the stronger animal who would lead the pack. But the human part bellowed internally that this beast would kill Aideen—his own pack member—without a single thought. The Griffin—the trained instinctual response within his dual mind—offered a solution that both man and beast could agree on.

As the Alpha dove from the balcony, Kieran dove for Aideen's submachine gun. Beast clashed with empty tile as Kieran rolled over his shoulder, grabbing the weapon, startling back Aideen, and spun on one knee. Holding the machine gun clumsily in one hand, he opened fire.

The shots sprayed wide, fired from a large, unsteady paw. The Alpha scrambled and dove away, charging into the nearby souvenir shop that was strafed by silver bullets. The Alpha roared as burning silver ripped through its shoulder and legs, but provided no clean kill shots.

The other werewolves that were prowling throughout the terminal responded and surged towards the battle with answering howls of their own.

The weapon clicked empty. Kieran turned and shoved the gun into Aideen's hands and fumbled to pull around the assault rifle slung across his shoulder. With a fleeting look of shock,

Aideen reloaded her weapon and pushed herself back up into Kieran's rear, covering his blind side.

"If you can hear me in there, Kieran, good fucking job," she said breathlessly. "Now let's finish the bastards!"

Kieran growled and charged forward to meet the coming werewolves. He fired wildly with his assault rifle, downing another werewolf as Aideen moved up alongside him. She covered the flanks, firing bursts at their rear and into the souvenir shop that the Alpha was still sulking in to keep it at bay.

A group of the werewolves mobbed Kieran at once, attacking from several angles—two from the upper balcony, three from ahead, one clambering up from the lower floor. He dropped his now empty assault rifle and threw Aideen under him, shielding her as his Griffin instincts told him to tap twice on the comms still wedged in his ear. It was a signal that the man on the receiving end would hopefully understand.

Even over the sound of swarming beasts, there was a cacophony of rattling hail that rose above it all. The upper window shattered as Lucas swooped around in the Hippogriff to open fire. The attacking werewolves were torn apart in a rain of silver fire as the atmosphere once again rushed to exit the terminal. Kieran grabbed the closest werewolf to him and used it as a meat shield against the deadly hail. It whined and yelped as it was torn in half under the onslaught. Lucas tracked the scrambling werewolves with his fire and Kieran hefted the disembodied torso of the dead werewolf by its wrist, using it as a meaty bludgeon.

Lucas's prolonged burst ceased as the majority of the remaining werewolves scattered to cover from overhead fire.

The rushing air was halted by another emergency shutter slamming into place where the pane used to be. In the sudden, ear ringing silence, Kieran charged forth with his new bloody weapon in tow, routing the scattered werewolves by swinging the shrivelling torso like a rag doll. Aideen picked herself up and gunned down the other stragglers who took cover from fire above, but not adequate cover from her.

A monstrous roar interrupted their slaughter and the Alpha exploded form the souvenir shop, yellow eyes cracked with bloodshot rage as it bounded for Kieran. Kieran threw the limp human torso at the Alpha, who deftly knocked it aside and it struck with a savage swipe at Kieran's neck. Kieran blocked it—flinching back under the force of the blow—but he managed to get a grapple hold on the Alpha's arm. Snarling, he spun and threw the Alpha over his shoulder. He kept a hold of its arm as he slammed it over a cafe table and twisted, dislocating the limb from its socket. The Alpha snarled in anger, tearing at Kieran's face with its free arm.

Aideen rushed in, jumping on top of the werewolf without fear, drawing her pistol and unloading it into the flailing Alpha's chest. It shuddered and trembled with each burning round and slowly stopped fighting against Kieran's hold—but not slowly enough. Aideen loaded her last magazine and fired into its chest again and again, until its only movement was from the jolting impacts of the silver bullets. It shrivelled slowly into a young man's shocked corpse.

Aideen rolled off the body on the table and collapsed onto her knees, panting. Kieran released the dead human and howled a monstrous roar—an Alpha roar—that rattled the heavy windows above. He sniffed and scanned the area with a snarl, scenting no more living werewolves, no more rivals, no more threats to his pack. The dank musk of werewolf was now tainted, dead, a sign that the cursed bodies were all transformed back to the fleshy humans they once were.

The human mind felt a pang of remorse for their fate, it was not their fault they were cursed, captured, and shipped to the Moon. The beast mind did not care; they were not his pack.

"Kieran," Aideen said hesitantly. Kieran turned to find her aiming the pistol right between his eyes. "Are you going to eat me?"

Kieran snarled at the threat as the cursed rage threatened to spill over. *My pack member is challenging me?* Aideen pulled the hammer back on the weapon with tears in her eyes.

"Want me to open up on him?" Lucas's voice crackled in Kieran's pointed ear. The mighty metal beast that was the Hippogriff swooped around one of the undamaged glass panes and Kieran turned to snarl at it.

Within, his mind was raging. *They are not threatening you! You are threatening them! Please, just calm down!* The beast within demanded respect, it demanded that they whimper back in fear and show deference. But the other voice within—the Griffin—sternly reminded man and beast both of the last remaining enemy in the terminal.

"No!" Aideen cried. "He's not like them, he . . . Kieran, can you understand me?"

Kieran snarled again, but not at Aideen. He turned, scenting the imposter that inhabited his den—Diondre. He scented blood and a tendril whiff of sweat infused with untrustworthy pheromones. How could they have ever trusted someone with such a scent? He bounded after Diondre, scrambling up a level and down the terminal.

As he bounded with a click-clack scraping gait across the terminal floor, civilians who were cautiously emerging from their hideouts cried out in terror and retreated back into relative safety. Their high pitched yelps and quick scurrying was like the sizzle of meat in the pan to Kieran's beast mind. Their scents of fear clung out to his snout like sweet, viscous honey.

But he had an imposter to disembowel.

He ignored the easy prey and followed the scent trail through the stalls and around the shops and up and down levels. All the while the pungency rose, and his bloodlust rose with it. But there were other sensations vying for attention, things that did not make sense to his beast mind, like the crackle in his ear of frantic pack mates on the comms.

The human mind interpreted some of it through the haze of the hunt, and the human mind communicated urgency.

"What do you mean?" Aideen's flustered voice buzzed. "It's your system, freeze him out."

"He has a master key code!" Gaz said.

"How did he get a master key?" Roshni inquired, "Out of the way, I might be able to block him out. The master key is an access code from Sigma Base. He's jerry rigged it into the terminal system, clever bastard."

"What is he even doing in the system? Kieran must be about to catch up to him by now," Aideen said.

"Emergency shutters." Lucas said.

"How did you know that?" Roshni replied, accompanied by the quick tip-tapping of furious typing.

"Because I can see the bloody things closing over the windows!"

"He's blocking you from tracking him then," Aideen was huffing.

"No . . . you said you injected Kieran with a serum, yes?" Roshni asked.

"What of it?" Aideen said.

"My contact at Sigma said it can reduce the werewolf transformation state when they're blocked from moonlight."

"Fuck me. Kieran, if you can hear me—fuck, if you can understand me—fall back. Diondre knows how to deal with you!"

But the prey was close. Kieran's human mind screamed for caution, the Griffin mind screamed to wait for backup, but both were muted as the beast mind screamed for blood.

Kieran bounded around a corner and found the imposter, the den infiltrator, the *prey* that had deemed itself predator. He was hunched up against the far wall, his wrist pad linked into an exposed circuit with his suit's visor flipped up. His dark brow creased and dripped with sweat as he swore and mumbled to himself. The whites of his eyes flickered and Kieran grinned wickedly. Diondre knew he was here, and pretending that he didn't wasn't going to save him.

Kieran howled and bounded forward.

The pale light from above winked out as the emergency shutters slammed shut over all the windows. The dim alarm lighting illuminated the eerie space with pulses of amber and flickers of dim red floor paths.

The beast mind quieted. Kieran could hear himself think again. But he urged his body forward despite the exhaustion creeping into his limbs. Just a few more paces . . . he just needed a second. Diondre finally responded to his presence, whipping out his silver spear and aiming it at the charging Kieran.

Training overrode instinct and Kieran ducked to the side, crashing through a stand of purses in a chaotic clutter. His lungs wheezed and his skin burned even though he was cold and shivering. His teeth ached like nothing he had ever experienced.

"Did he get me?" Kieran worked his numb jaw, feeling at it with a fleshy hand full of limp muscle. "That's not a good sign." Kieran struggled out of the mess of bags and shelves, crawling as if half dead—he was so tired.

The click clacking approach of magnetic boots stopped him as he emerged. He looked up, Diondre now stood over him with the unfired silver spear. "I gotta tell ya, Kieran, I didn't think I would ever shit myself." His professional demeanour had turned sour; the veil was lifted.

"I ain't done with you yet, prick," Kieran panted, trying to struggle up onto all fours. "I'm sure there'll be plenty more shit to squeeze out of you before I'm through." Kieran reached for his pistol.

Diondre laughed. He kicked the pistol out of Kieran's hand and it clattered across the floor. He raised the silver spear, aiming at the defenceless Griffin, and squeezed the trigger. It whined as the gasses built up in the chamber. Kieran only had a second to act, and if he could just dodge to the side, reach out, do anything . . . but he was so tired.

"Just so you know," Diondre said, "this isn't personal."

"I don't care what you think," Kieran mumbled, scrunching his eyes shut.

There was a whistle and a loud spark. Kieran flinched back, his chest seizing as he drew his last breath, only to realise he was still alive.

He looked up and Diondre was staggering, holding a half shattered silver spear in his hands with a shocked, idiotic expression. Kieran followed his bewildered gaze and found his saviour. Aideen was sprawled on the ground after hopping down a balcony and was holding her smoking pistol in both hands.

"Hands off my sergeant!" Her slide was locked back—empty—she discarded the weapon and drew her knife.

Diondre recovered and bolted down the terminal corridor, to the long travelators that led to the hangar.

"He's out of firepower!" Kieran cried as Aideen scrambled up and sprinted towards him.

"Me too—are you okay?"

"Don't stop for me, get him!"

AIDEEN KELLY

Aideen didn't break stride as she sped past Kieran and onto the travelators after Diondre. He took one with directional markings pointing towards the hangar and Aideen took the other one—they weren't working, of course, so it made no difference. The only things that seemed to be working in this accursed place were the emergency lighting, the life support, and the magnetic flooring.

As her click-clack magnetic humming slammed down onto the segmented conveyor belt, Aideen had an idea.

"Roshni, are you in control of the system yet?" she panted.

"Kinda—he did a number on the network on his way in. What do you need?"

"Access his suit's magnetic frequency. Lock him down!"

"On it." The travelators spanned two hundred meters and Diondre was halfway down them when Roshni's voice buzzed in Aideen's ear again. "I'm locking down his boots—now!"

There was a loud click and Diondre swore as he stumbled forward, only stopping from falling and breaking his legs by grabbing onto the rubber travelator railing. The only problem was Aideen had the same reaction as her boots also locked into place.

"Roshni, what the fuck?" Aideen spat, grimacing as her injured leg tweaked again.

"I'm sorry, I'm sorry, I'm working on it!"

Aideen yelled at the top of her lungs in frustration. Diondre was ten metres in front of her and she couldn't do a thing about it.

He laughed and keyed the team's comms. "This is what happens when you send the Pantheon."

"Screw you, Diondre!" Roshni replied.

"Just get me out of this, Roshni." Aideen was trying to unbuckle her boots but they were sealed tight with the mag lock.

"I'm trying, but I can't free your boots without shutting down the magnetic flooring of the entire section. He'll be free too. Just—wait for backup."

Diondre was wriggling, trying to look back at Aideen. "Though, the incompetence of the Pantheon is nothing compared to the thorn in your side that the Griffins are. You lot really know how to throw a spanner into an already FUBAR situation. Still, you did impressive work, Aideen. Are you sure you wouldn't rather serve the greater good, the natural order of things?"

"Don't listen to him, Aideen!" Roshni said.

"Of course I'm not going to listen to him!" Aideen spat. In front of her, Diondre started tearing off his moon suit. "Shit." Aideen realised what he realised—that his boots were a part of his suit, not separately locked and sealed on like hers were. If he could loosen them and wriggle out of his suit, he could get away. "Roshni, he's going to get free! Unlock the floor."

"It'll take time."

"I don't have time!" Aideen looked around helplessly for anything to help her. Gazing down at her locked boots in frustration, she had another idea. "Can you turn on the travelator?"

"I think so?"

"Do it. Reverse both travelator directions and turn them on."

"Okay."

The travelators lurched into reverse motion, Diondre lurching towards Aideen as she lurched towards him.

He stopped fumbling with his suit and drew a knife. She had the advantage in this bout as his back was to her, but she had to focus; she had to make it count. She tensed and relaxed the grip on her knife as she waited for the humming travelators to bring them within arm's reach.

"Trust a Griffin to try and kill me with a slow motion joust," Diondre grimaced.

"It won't be slow enough," Aideen spat.

They came within swiping distance, slowly, painfully. Aideen went for the easy strike, swiping at Diondre's midsection. He wrenched himself around to parry her blow, cramping the muscles in his sides from the contortionist effort, and only managed to redirect the slicing impact down his hip, biting into the padding of his space suit.

Aideen continued her attack unperturbed, and stabbed this time into Diondre's shoulder blades, but he wildly whipped his knife at her head and she was forced to duck before she could thrust. They passed by each other, facing side on now, and Aideen recovered from the exchange before Diondre. She snapped her knife out at shoulder height, the blade glanced off the neck lock where his visor would seal in place and deflected downwards into his suit, biting into the nape of his neck.

Diondre cried out and flinched away, tripping as his feet were still locked in place and collapsing awkwardly onto the trundling railing.

"Roshni, stop the travelators," Aideen ordered. They trundled a few more metres before humming to a halt, and Diondre's attempts to recover were hindered by his shifting momentum. "Unlock our boots."

Roshni muttered over the comms for a moment as she tried to comply. Finally, Aideen's boots unlocked from the travelator's surface, as did Diondre's.

He collapsed onto the floor and Aideen hopped over the dividing railings lightly, like a dancer on wires. She bounded to where Diondre was slumped, putting pressure on his neck to try and stop the bleeding. He pointed his knife at her wearily with his free hand.

"Stay back," he said.

Aideen kicked his blade away. It flung out across the far side of the travelator corridor, spinning endlessly in the low-G. She flipped her knife under hand and impaled his hand into the rubber railing. Diondre cried out again but was stifled as Aideen grabbed his neck, adding more pressure over his other hand to the wound. The small jet of blood spraying through his fingers halted.

"You've got some explaining to do," Aideen said, baring her teeth. She fumbled through his pouches, looking for the data Helena gave him at Sigma. She pulled it out with bloody fingers and pocketed it.

"It doesn't matter," Diondre murmured, his dark skin growing pale and cold, his eyes losing focus. "He will rise."

"Who?"

"The false gods will be overthrown and the world will return to its natural state."

"What the fuck are you on about? Who will be overthrown? What natural state?"

Diondre coughed and spluttered. "Careful who you trust there, Griffin." His eyes turned dull and his grip weakened around his neck. He breathed one last ragged gasp and his body shuddered as he died.

"Sod it." Aideen pulled the knife out of the now dead hand and wiped it on her suit before sheathing it. "Kieran!" she moon skipped down the terminal travelator.

She found Kieran slumped against a glass balcony railing. He was half comatose and half naked, having torn off his tactical vest and tattered suit. His head lolled as his chest heaved with every breath.

"Kieran," Aideen skidded to her knees as she got closer, gracefully sliding to a halt next to him and taking his face in her hands. "Kieran, are you awake?"

He mumbled incoherently.

Aideen looked him over, checking for wounds, her eyes flitting over his barely visible scar lines from his infection. His breath was raspy and she tore her helmet off, placing her ear on his chest.

"It burns," he wheezed.

Aideen jumped back in fright, but regained herself, "What burns?"

"I think I got some silver in my lungs back there, plus I still feel like I was spaced, and my joints and muscles ache like I've had a bad flu. Basically I just feel not very nice all over." He grinned weakly and his head lolled again.

Aideen kept him steady. "Kieran, focus. If the silver smoke was going to kill you it would have done so by now. It'll just be a little uncomfortable while you cough it up. As for the aches, I'm sure it's not easy transforming. We should get you to the Hippogriff." She keyed her comms, "Lucas."

"I hear ya, swinging down to the hangar now. Is the area clear?"

"All hostiles neutralised," Aideen responded.

"Ten-four, I'll be with ya with a medical kit and a stretcher, ASAP."

"No." Kieran mumbled.

"What was that?" Aideen said.

Kieran pushed something into Aideen's hands, the pistol Diondre had kicked from his grasp. "You promised."

"But Kieran, you're not like the other ones."

"I almost was. I'm a monster, Aideen—cursed, a paranormal threat. End me."

"I won't . . ."

"Corporal!" Kieran snarled, his face contorting into a foul, horrific grimace for only a second. Aideen jumped to her feet, aiming the pistol in one swift motion at her friend's head. "Good." Kieran wheezed. "Now just one more thing to do."

"You snarled like that on purpose, didn't you?" Aideen's voice wavered. "Trying to make things easier on me, huh?"

"You always needed your hand held." Kieran smiled weakly.

"Wanker," Aideen forced a smile as her face glistened with tears.

The hammer on the pistol tilted back as she squeezed the trigger, steeling herself to keep her aim steady.

"Wait!"

Aideen rolled between Kieran and the voice and held her weapon at the ready, aiming at Roshni, who was sprinting towards them.

"You better keep your distance there, pilot," Aideen spat.

"You don't need to kill him." Roshni held her hands out in surrender as she stumbled to a halt. "With the serum injected, my organisation can help rehabilitate him."

"What organisation, the fucking Sect?"

"No, we oppose the Sect."

"What does that even mean? Who the hell are you? Start talking or I'm going to put one in your gut and let you bleed out."

Roshni bit her lip. "Okay, okay. Sigma Base had a scientist embedded from my organisation, the Pantheon. His name was

Doctor Felix Hernandez. He had suspicions that the Sect was going to make a move for their research. He sent that intel a week ago. That was around the same time your team was ambushed by Sect forces and your squad mate Jason was killed. We suspected your squad would be called out to the Moon if Sigma was compromised, seeing as you were the only Griffins on the roster at the orbital spire. So we fudged some paperwork, made sure your co-pilot Monica was kept in the hospital for observation so I could infiltrate your team and keep tabs on things. But by then, Diondre had already been selected as a transfer. I had no way of knowing if it was him who had infiltrated your unit, or if it was already infiltrated by a long time member."

"So you were only supposed to keep tabs on things?" Aideen asked.

Roshni hesitated. "I was supposed to sabotage the Hippogriff if I believed Sect forces got a hold of the research. I was supposed to sabotage all inter-planetary vessels. I changed tack when the werewolves breached the terminal. Please—the Sect says they're striving towards the greater good. But their greater good involves catastrophe. The Pantheon is all that stands in their way, and it has been that way since the ancient times."

"How can we trust you? How come the Griffins don't know shit about this?" the gun in Aideen's hand was quivering.

"The United Globe government has only been around a few decades. Every country before then had their counter-paranormal teams. They dealt with basic threats, small scale battles. But the Pantheon has always fought the war in secret, behind the scenes. Just because most of the world's governments united doesn't mean that secrecy suddenly changes."

"Aideen," Kieran rasped. "Her scent—I can't explain it, but she's telling the truth."

"But it doesn't make any fucking sense, Kieran!"

Magnetic footsteps caught their attention and Roshni and Aideen both turned on the figure bounding down the travelator corridor. It was Lucas, with a medical hover gurney in tow.

"Whoa!" He clicked to a halt and raised his hands. "Hey, it's just me."

"Lucas. Let's get the sergeant out of here," Roshni said.

"And go where?" Aideen aimed back at Roshni.

"Yeah, we have three other Hippogriffs dispatched from Command," Lucas said. "They'll be here in half a day for clean up."

"Some of them may very well have Sect agents." Roshni said. "If we leave now I can get us somewhere safe."

"And what about us? We'd be classified AWOL," Aideen said. "You expect us to risk everything on your word," she glanced at Kieran who had slipped into unconsciousness again, "or your . . . smell?"

Roshni smiled. "You may be surprised."

Part 9: Drafted

AIDEEN KELLY

Aideen and Lucas stood in their standard Griffin fatigues in the hangar of a facility constructed from blue steel. They were armed and bleary eyed. Floof sat next to them, wagging his tail and panting.

"It's hecking windy out there!" he barked.

Aideen scratched his head, "I know, boy, stay close."

Roshni was with them too, unarmed and wearing a navy blue jumpsuit and holding a data pad. Next to her was the facility's chief science officer, a petite woman in a lab coat with blonde hair pulled into a ponytail and large spectacles.

The door to the hangar groaned open, revealing a torrential downpour outside and lashings of great lightning. A Hippogriff loomed from the storm, setting down by the welcome party. As the loading bay doors lowered, Aideen and Lucas exchanged glances. Standing at the top of the loading bay ramp were three people, one of whom they recognised instantly. General Xing—the highest ranking member of Griffin Command—stood tall in his black and bronze dress uniform with both hands behind his back. Of the other two with him, one was a Griffin Commander that they didn't recognise and the other was a pale, lithe man in the same blue jumpsuit that Roshni was wearing.

"Lieutenant Deans, Corporal Kelly, good evening," General Xing said.

"Are you two not going to salute?" the commander next to him asked. He had deep umber skin and a thick African accent.

"You'll have to forgive them, Commander," Roshni said. "Since they've been here they've slept in shifts, always kept their weapons with them and have only eaten from the stores in their Hippogriff."

Xing's serious expression was mired by a sly smile. "Griffins will be Griffins. Stand down, Commander, they've been through a bit."

"Yes, General," the commander said.

"Ah, General . . ." Aideen said, trying to squint and blink the sleep out of her eyes.

"What Aideen here means, sir," Lucas interrupted, "is what the fuck?"

"You don't think that the Griffins were started by some competent global government do you?" Xing replied with a laugh. "Not at all, they started the same way that all of the paranormal organisations started, through Pantheon influence."

"So," Aideen rubbed her brow, exhaustion having taken hold days ago, "we can trust them, we can trust you?"

"I was a Pantheon agent before the Griffins were even a thing, Corporal."

"All right then," Lucas gestured to the man in the blue jumpsuit with them. "Then who's this smug looking bastard?"

"I," the man raised his hand and an electrical charge swept through Lucas's gun. Lucas yelped and dropped it as the man continued, "Am a story for another time. For now, call me

Brecca. Your victory over the Sect in this matter has made them rash. They are making more blatant moves and we must act quickly. Where is this Sergeant Ahmad?"

"This way," the chief science officer gestured, leading them from the hangar and through blue steel corridors. She had a soft, airy voice.

"General, sir," Aideen said as they marched. "What is the Sect? What is the Pantheon? No one here has told us anything."

"There is much to discuss, and you would believe very little of it," Xing said as they came to a large vault with warning signs and two heavily armed guards in blue jumpsuits on either side of the door. "The Cronos Sect is a group of fanatics who are trying to break the Titan Cronos from his prison."

"Heh," Lucas said. "Damn, that sleep deprivation really does you in. Cronos? As in the father of the gods? I must be losing it."

Brecca grunted and shook his head. "Your myths are but children's tales of a time before history; they are rife with fantasy and full of errors. But in essence, yes. Why else do you think the people who oppose them are called the Pantheon, little human?"

Aideen and Lucas fell dead silent as the atmosphere pricked at their skin. Brecca seemed to possess his space in the corridor with more than just his body.

"Ah . . ." Lucas opened his mouth to speak but faltered.

"Sod that," Aideen said, finding her resolve. "I've seen cosmic fuckery without going mad, I've wrangled with banshees and I'm still here to bitch about it. You're just some guy with a buzzer in your pocket."

Brecca turned his gaze to her, his smile hardening into a glare without so much as a tweak in his facial muscles. Aideen clenched her fist, staring back with all of her might.

"You don't have very much respect, little one." His pale skin slipped through different spectrums of light, a phenomenon that Aideen was aware of yet could not wholly observe.

"I lost my whole team fighting blind against your enemies, you gobshite. A lack of respect is the least of your worries from me."

"Brecca," Xing said sternly, "they did not become Griffins for their formality."

Brecca relaxed from challenging Aideen, who clenched her jaw to stop her teeth from chattering.

Lucas placed his hand on her shoulder and squeezed. "I always knew you had bigger balls than me."

Aideen stifled a nervous chuckle.

"Guards," the chief science officer said, "would you open the doors please?"

"Doctor, he is currently in a state of metamorphosis," the guard warned with disinterest.

"Just do it, kid," the commander said.

The guard wordlessly keyed the door to hiss open. Floof charged through the widening opening into a large, dark space, barking madly.

"Does the dog annoy him?" Xing asked as the group entered. The room was lit only by the hallway behind them.

"I think he considers it a part of his pack," Roshni replied. "With those he considers not to be a part of his pack . . . I just wouldn't make any sudden moves."

"Noted."

Floof stayed at the edge of the light, barking incessantly, his collar shouting "Fren!" over and over again.

The room smelled of wet dog and body odour. Something in the dark growled, revealing teeth lit by what little light spilled in from the hallway. It leered at them with yellow eyes surrounded by pale rings of light. The werewolf prowled into sight, its long dark claws clicking upon the flooring and it towered over the barking dog, reaching out for its neck . . .

It nuzzled Floof and started to wrestle with him.

Aideen laughed and stepped forward, prodding at the brawling mass of fur, "Kieran, we need you to be able to talk to us!"

The werewolf snarled at Aideen but did not strike. Instead it grabbed her by the shoulders and pulled her into the playful brawl with a startled cry.

"Will he not curse her?" Xing asked.

"No, sir," the science officer said. "He seems to be able to not slice and dice people he considers friendly."

"I'm still not wrestling with him," Lucas laughed. "But I'm glad he's on our side."

Xing stepped forward. "Sergeant."

Kieran looked up from the brawl and snarled, stepping forward quickly onto his hind legs and towering over the general. The two guards from the hallway rushed in, but Roshni ushered them back with a wave of her hand.

Aideen climbed to her feet and dusted the shed fur from her uniform as Kieran slowly reached up to the rings of pale light surrounding his yellow eyes. He peeled them from his face. They were a strange pair of goggles.

"They have moon chalk lining the rims with accompanying UV lights." The chief science officer explained to Brecca and the commander. "He can activate them to engage in a controlled metamorphosis. The more time he spends as a werewolf, the more he seems to be able to control it. He describes it like having two minds, beast and man. He has to constantly try to convince the beast mind to act in alignment with what the man mind wants. The serum helped, but it's his discipline—well, he says his faith—that helps him remain mostly in control."

"You're saying it's divine intervention?" the commander asked, raising an eyebrow.

"He doesn't describe it like that," she answered. "He uses his faith as a grounding rod. In essence, it's something to help focus on his humanity. That helps the human mind, in his words, to suggest things to the beast mind."

"Sounds tenuous," Brecca said.

As the scientist explained the situation, Kieran slowly shrivelled into his smaller—but still large for a human—form. He was panting, glistening with a layer of sweat, and had clumps of shed fur clinging to his skin. He almost doubled over in exhaustion, but rallied and remained steady.

"General Xing," he said, and saluted. "It's good to see you again."

"I must say, Kieran, after I found you, arm deep in werewolf guts all those years ago, I never thought I'd see you like this."

"It was not my choice, sir."

"I understand. It has been an unfortunate time. But I must ask more of you now, you and your remaining team."

"Whatever it is, sir, we'll get it done."

"I want you to enter the war."

"What war, sir?"

"The war between gods and titans."

The Science Myth Saga will continue with the next instalment:

The Dragon Roost on the Orbital Spire

A note from the author

Thanks for reading!

If you enjoyed this, please consider leaving a review. Leaving reviews is one of the best ways to support your favourite authors. The second best thing you can do is recommend their stuff to your friends!

My mission is to write kickass stories, with inspiring and relatable characters for all Sci-Fi and Fantasy readers to enjoy. I appreciate you coming along for the ride.

To find an up to date list of **my available BOOKS**[1] you can check out my website www.seanmts.com[2] and head to the books tab. While you're there you can also read free flash + serial fiction that I post regularly.

If you ever want to get in contact, you can email me: sean@seanmts.com

You can sign up to my mailing list[3] through my website to get a **FREE Sci-Fi novelette** and stay up to date on my future releases.

You could also connect with me on social media.

Facebook: Sean M. T. Shanahan[4]

Instagram: @seanmtshanahan[5]

Twitter: @seanmts[6]

I am always keen to answer questions, or just have yarn.

All the best, be at peace with your beast mind,

---

1.   **https://seanmts.com/books/**

2.   https://seanmts.com/

3.   https://seanmts.com/contact/

4.   https://www.facebook.com/SeanMTShanahan/

5.   https://www.instagram.com/seanmtshanahan/

6.   https://twitter.com/SeanMTS/status/1398938329698037761

Sean M. T. Shanahan

About the Author

Sean works as a Tour Guide in Sydney, Australia. He has always enjoyed storytelling and considers himself to be a huge nerd, especially when it comes to Fantasy, Sci-Fi and History. The natural path from there was to combine those interests and write his own stories, which he started in 2015.

When he isn't scribbling down his whacky ideas or finding the worst pun in order to make his friends groan, he spends his time training in Parkour (in the hopes he will one day become an urban ninja).

Also by Sean M. T. Shanahan

The Science Myth Saga
Werewolves In Space
Dragon Roost On The Orbital Spire

The Symbicate
The Symbicate
The Symbicate 2 - Attack Of The Light Wizards
The Symbicate 3 - The Beast In The Void

Printed in Australia
Ingram Content Group Australia Pty Ltd
AUHW012104061123
386100AU00007B/97